Dr. Watson's
American
Adventure

AIRSHIP 27 PRODUCTIONS

Interior illustrations © 2012 Pedro Cruz
Cover illustration © 2012 Rob Davis and Shane Evans

Managing Editor: Ron Fortier
Associate Editor: Ray Riethmeier
Production and design by Rob Davis.

Published by
Airship 27 Productions
www.airship27.com
www.airship27hangar.com

ISBN-13: 978-0615631295
ISBN-10: 0615631290

Printed in the United States of America

10 9 8 7 6 5 4 3 2 1

Dr. Watson's American Adventure
Contents:

Dr. Watson's American Adventure

by
Erwin K. Roberts

I t was just over two weeks after *The Adventure of the Empty House*. I had begun the procedures for selling my small medical practice and seeing to the storage of that which could not be moved back to Baker Street. For at the invitation of Mr. Sherlock Holmes, I was headed there again.

I felt a strange duality as I prepared to leave the quarters I'd shared with my late wife. Memories of our happiness lingered there, but those same memories told me I would be far less melancholy living back at 221B. As the evening approached I was very relieved when someone knocked on my door.

"Dr. Watson?" asked the roughly dressed young man. I judged him to be about fourteen. I acknowledged that I was indeed Dr. Watson. An envelope was placed in my hand. Before I could ask a question, or offer a coin, he dashed off.

Then I heard two laughing words drift back to me from his path in the street, "Irregular delivery." A message from Holmes. What else could it have been? Barely back in London and the man had the young Baker Street Irregulars in operation. I tore open the envelope.

"My Dear Watson," read the scrap of paper inside.

"A small crate was delivered for you while I was out attending to matters. (I presume this means that the city directory has received your request to change your address.) While not marked as such, I perceive that said crate came from America, and in all probability was delivered by the crew of the ship it on which it arrived.

"Unless this is something you arranged yourself, I assume you will want to open it soonest. Therefore I have asked Mrs. Hudson to set two places for dinner.

"Yours, etc.,"

The initials "S.H." followed. And soon I rode in a cab to Baker Street.

Holmes must have had an unproductive time that day. For he rose and came over to the item as I entered. "You identified the source of the wood, no doubt," I said.

"Of course, Watson. Such as any carpenter in New England might have lying about his shop. The address was correct when shipped, but is followed by instruction to check it against the City Directory. What passes for a return address intrigues me. A caricature of a face was traced into the upper left board, then darkened by an artist's pencil. Finally a coat of Shellac preserved it. Though roughly copied, the drawing seems to be the work of Thomas Nast, the political cartoonist."

As he spoke, I hung up my hat and stick to join him. One glance at the drawing told me the sender. "A boisterous, but still very serious fellow. At least on many subjects dear to your heart, Holmes. Last year we shared some very good and very dangerous times together. My wife enjoyed his company, though not the dangerous times. We returned to these shores feeling we understood much more about America than before. That was just a few weeks before she became ill."

"So sorry to have brought that part of things to mind, my dear fellow. But you intrigue me. Adventures in America? Of what sort? Please, I have had a deadly dull day. Dull week, for that matter. For a change you can regal me with tales of your doings. *Mrs. Hudson!* You may serve now!"

So that evening Mr. Sherlock Holmes listened while I recounted my visit to the United States of America.

***

The affair started as some of your cases, Holmes. The business card and note, followed by a very private visitor. I was in my consulting room when a liveried messenger service boy appeared. He offered me a sealed packet, taking care to show the seals fully intact. Intrigued, and remembering your methods, I asked him how he came by the thing.

"It's what we call a 'round-a-bout', sir. Keeps the sender very private, it does. Somebody gives a big packet and money to a street boy. He brings it to a messenger service, pays the delivery fee. The change pays the boy. The thing's addressed to another service. When it arrives at the second service, they open it. Inside is their fee to deliver what's inside. I've heard tell of parcels going to every service in the whole of London before the day's done. Can't say who else might've touched it, sir. My orders are to come back in an hour for your answer."

Taking care to preserve the seals for later study I opened the thing. Inside was a formal double enveloped letter on the stationary of the firm of well respected solicitors whom I'm sure you know by reputation. The letter was signed by the senior partner himself. It read:

My Dear Dr. Watson,

Please forgive the melodrama surrounding this missive. My client has asked that every precaution be taken to insure your privacy in this matter. So much so that even I do not yet know the actual subject. Let me simply say that my client is of a prominent American family. A man whose reputation for honesty and fair dealing is totally unchallenged.

My client wishes me to meet both with you and your wife. At that time I shall deliver to you a sealed letter. Then I shall try to answer any questions you may have. Or find such additional information as you may request. My client also states that he has no objection whatever should you desire to have representatives of the police in attendance. (Apparently he is aware, as am I, of your relationship with the late Mr. Sherlock Holmes and the possible danger that might still entail.)

I hold myself at your convenience this evening. Should that not be possible, please give the messenger a time and place. He will telegraph your reply to a private address the firm maintains.

Yours Sincerely,

Artemus H. Legendre

Fortune stood with me that afternoon as I was immediately able to reach Mr. Peter Jones, one of the few members of the police who truly values your methods. With Jones invited to sup with Mary and myself, I gave the returning messenger a positive reply and a good tip.

After a fine plain cooked meal, Jones proposed a toast to your memory. Hardly had we finished that when Mr. Legendre arrived. Fortunately, he and Peter Jones had met on business a time or two. I positively brimmed with curiosity during the pleasantries, including a fine glass of port.

Finally Mr. Legendre opened the slim case he carried. He passed me a well sealed packet. The inscription read, in part: "To be delivered by hand to Doctor John H. Watson, MD, late of Her Majesty's 5th Northumberland Fusiliers...." The gist of the writing made delivery to any other John Watson and wife Mary virtually impossible.

Legendre reached for his pen-knife, but Jones beat him to the draw, as it were. I am certain he possessed near as much curiosity about the matter as I.

A moment later I removed a letter from the packet. After a quick glance at its contents I read it aloud.

My Dear Dr. Watson,
(And please consider your wife Mary included in this salutation.)

I do not intend this to sound as if I mainly write to you because I admire *your* writing. But I have indeed enjoyed your stories of Sherlock Holmes from the drawing rooms of Manhattan to the campfires in God's Wonder that is Yellowstone in our far west.

On my last journey west I happened to find a copy of the one of your accounts that had thus far eluded my eyes. Near the small town of Deadwood, in the Dakotas, I chanced upon *The Sign of the Four*. I read it, as obviously had many others, while waiting out the end of a major blizzard. After finishing, I discovered that the Nighthawk (an Americanism for a cattle ranch's night watchman.) of the S-Bar-F ranch shared the family name of your wife's birth.

Morstan being a far from common name, at least on this side of the Atlantic, I brought this to Mr. Ashley Morstan's attention. The fellow expressed surprise when I made him aware of what you had written about Mrs. Watson's father. He half remembered hearing tales during his youth that seemed to fit in with what you had written about the family. At the end of my stay, the snow having melted, Mr. Morstan freely gave me the names of some family members living in, of all places, upstate New York.

Upon my return east I had town records quietly checked. Members of a family named Morstan do indeed live in and around the town of Warrensburg in the Adirondack mountain area of my home State.

Now, sir, I realize that you may have changed your wife's maiden name in your manuscript prior to publication. And even if not, you may have reason not to want this particular pot to be stirred. Therefore I write this letter to you.

I have enclosed with this letter all the information I currently possess in this matter. Should you wish me to drop the matter, consider it done. Should you be interested in knowing more, you have but to tell me how to proceed. And, on the chance you wish to look into the issue personally, I should be most happy to act as your host and guide.

Yours Respectfully, and Most Sincerely,

Theodore Roosevelt
Gramercy Park, New York City

I shan't bore you with details of the rest of the meeting. We four discussed the general situation. Legendre told me what he could of this Mr. Roosevelt, and he gave me the cable address of his corresponding law firm in the city of New York. I had little thought at that point beyond dispatching a telegram to thank Mr. Roosevelt for his kind interest, and his discretion.

As we prepared to retire for the night, Mary came to me saying, "My dear John. Having a family again, even at this distance, would be wonderful. And, my husband, the opportunity to be away from London would do you so much good. With Sherlock Holmes gone, you need to step away from him and his work. And that is no disloyalty to him, or his memory. Here is a possible mystery you are well able to investigate. Please John, let us go to America."

She was indeed correct, my friend, for it seemed that I saw you and your work wherever I chanced to be in London. On that corner we met a person involved in a particular case. Something strange going on down that alley. I wonder what Holmes would have made of it. Lestrade caught the blighter straightaway. Holmes might have had a compliment for him. And so on.

It took Mary to make me realize that I was suffocating, like walking in a yellow pea-soup fog. Save for her and my patients all seemed at a standstill in my life. Much as I hated long sea voyages, a trip to the New World would be as a blood transfusion to a man with seeping veins.

The following morning I dispatched a brief telegram to Mr. Roosevelt stating that Mary and I had some interest in traveling to America, but were concerned about putting too much a burden upon his hospitality. Just over thirty hours later his reply reached my hand.

"Burden on Hospitality? Nonsense!" read the paper I held. "My friends visiting Europe of late say that the liner American Star is the fastest to New York. She sails from Southampton in a fortnight. Or inform me of another choice."

"A very direct man," commented Holmes.

"You have no idea, my friend, but I feel I must mention what Mr. Legendre told me. The spelling of the family name would indicate that the first syllable should be pronounced like the word 'rose.' However, this particular Roosevelt insists on pronouncing the thing as in the end of the word 'kangaroos.'"

The timing of the American Star's sailing did indeed seem right. I booked second class passage. Then Mary and I began to prepare for the journey in earnest. I visited the offices of the Strand Magazine to learn what I could about those legally publishing my stories across the Atlantic.

A mistake, that, as you will become aware. They did agree to run my observations of America in the Strand, or find a place for my dispatches in a travel magazine. I hoped to partially offset our expenses in this manner.

I outfitted as I had done for one of Her Majesty's Army transports. I would return home laden with various things that my good wife would then tell me were provided, or would be available, if needed on board.

Mr. Roosevelt and I helped make the cable companies a bit wealthier with our correspondence. Now that he knew of our interest, I would dispatch a telegram first thing in the morning. In spite of the time difference I sometimes received a reply just after noon, and always long before dinner.

One unusual event occurred during that period. Mary and I received a letter from New York. It read:

My Dear Dr. and Mrs. Watson,

I am Anna, Theodore Roosevelt's sister. I look forward to your visit.

My brother approaches having you two as house guests as he does most things. That being Full Steam Ahead. He must have a dozen tentative plans to lay before you concerning Mrs. Watson's family and seeing what of our city, state, and nation you may care to.

However, there is one thing that I feel I should make you aware of. On February 12th of 1884, Theodore's daughter Alice was born. Two days later, on the 14th, her mother, also named Alice, and our own mother both passed away each within hours of the other.

Naturally my brother was devastated. Young Alice has been in my care since then. My brother's only way to deal with the loss of his wife has been to totally remove her from his life. As if she never existed. Had he not done so, I fear the intensity of his sorrow would have destroyed him.

Therefore, I must request that you never ask questions about Alice Lee Roosevelt of any member of our household.

Beyond this one thing, please accept our family's hospitality. I am sure we will all enjoy our time together.

Yours Most Sincerely,

Anna

The letter came with the first delivery of the day. Mary and I both read it. By unspoken agreement we put the matter aside until mid-afternoon.

Then Mary broke her silence on the matter.

"John, I can understand Mr. Roosevelt in the matter of his wife. In the years my father was missing I hardly dared to think of him. To imagine him alive would have raised false hope to be dashed again and again when he did not appear. To presume him dead would have cast me into the very abyss that Anna believes waited for her brother."

My thoughts on the matter ran much the same. Grateful to Mr. Roosevelt's sister we put the matter from our minds.

After that, the days went fairly swiftly. Steamer trunks sent ahead and confirmed aboard, we headed for Southampton and our embarkation for the "new" world. Mr. Peter Jones saw us off, stating that he felt he had a small personal interest in our venture.

On that day near the vernal equinox of the Year of Our Lord Eighteen-Hundred-and-Ninety-Two, our ship weighed anchor for the City of New York.

***

During the whole period before our embarkation I endeavored to learn more about Mr. Theodore Roosevelt. Some chaps at the American Embassy showed me copies of the New York Social Register and found some newspaper stories that mentioned him. I also took it upon myself to reach out to your brother, Mycroft. Since your supposed passing I had only tendered my regrets and condolences along with a formal report of all that I knew about the situation. I was unsure if he would respond to what could well be a too painful reminder of his loss.

You have referred to him as a repository of information, Holmes, and your brother proved it to me on that occasion. I sent out my request with the first post of the day. At mid-afternoon came a letter of multiple pages summarizing the public life of Theodore Roosevelt. I venture he dictated the missive to one of the staff at the Diogenes Club. Though fully understandable, several marks upon the paper suggested that the document was created in a single draft, rather than a basic one followed by the traditional fair copy. I shall show it to you some day. I'm afraid today it is buried in the preparations for the move.

Not long after the letter, and much to my astonishment, a runner from the Admiralty arrived. The grizzled senior Boatswain gave me the loan of a book Theodore Roosevelt began writing while still an undergraduate at Harvard College. The man told me that the book was considered the most objective and unbiased account of the Naval actions in existence of what the Americans call the War of 1812. War colleges on both sides of the Atlantic use and recommend it.

***

Mary and I waved our good-byes, and, as did many others, stayed by the ship's rails until land disappeared from view. We filled what remained of the day exploring those portions of the large liner as were open to us. Our cabin seemed positively spacious to me compared to the quite cramped conditions of Her Majesty's Royal Transport ships.

Mary quickly made acquaintance of many of our fellow passengers of several nations. Soon, as we plunged into the ship's social life, I realized just how much I had shut myself away after losing you, my dear Holmes. Mary did not prod me forward, so much as she led me out of a portion of my doldrums.

More often than I liked such feelings returned when various people realized that I was indeed **that** Dr. Watson. On the afternoon of our second full day out from Southampton, one of the men at our table in the lounge mentioned "your friend, Sherlock Holmes." He made the mistake to say that just as the steward refreshed his coffee. The poor fellow froze in surprise. And our acquaintance nearly had his entire groin area anointed by scalding liquid.

Obviously the steward mentioned what he heard. As Mary and I returned from playing whist that evening we found the ship's First Officer waiting outside our cabin. To Mary's delight, and my total astonishment, we found ourselves invited to a private breakfast with the Captain and other senior members of the crew.

In the morning an escort waited outside our door. In what a ship of war would call the Ward Room, I believe, waited most of the ships officers and one member of the steamship company's Board of Directors who happened to be making the crossing. Every soul present an avid follower of my accounts of your cases. In addition to the fine meal, I found myself being asked to sign publications carrying my stories. And in several languages other than English, as well. I felt a lump in my throat at the end when the Captain thanked me for his pleasure in reading the stories. He added thanks from both himself, and the line, for providing entertainment for both crew and passengers. Help in passing time was invaluable, he said. Then fine brandy was distributed. And the Captain led us in a toast to your memory, Holmes. The whole affair left my head in a mental fog for most of the day.

One thing the Captain hit spot on was passing the time, especially for passengers. In all but the most severe weather these steam liners plow ahead with great monotony. Sunrise and sunset aside, the thrill of 'sailing' seems nil. I fear I would have been far better entertained by a sea journey as a passenger in the age of sail. Then officers and seamen used their knowledge, instincts, and skills to wring both safety, and the last knot possible, from raw nature herself.

But time did pass, and pleasurably, for the most part. Toward the end of the last morning of the crossing we saw the land of the New World.

As we approached New York harbor the stewards kept up a dialog of the sights we approached and passed. Particular attention was paid to the so-called Statue of Liberty. You remember the Times carried quite a bit about the monument's dedication in 1886, Holmes.

Soon after we passed our closest to that remarkable sight we were approached by the Chief Purser of our sailing class. He asked that we accompany him to the bridge of the ship.

The docking of a ship being possibly the most stressful time of the whole passage, I began to fear that some trouble awaited us. After a manner it did.

The Captain greeted us in a cordial, if distracted manner. He then turned us over to the Second Officer whom we had met previously. That chap took us into a small compartment directly behind the bridge itself. There he showed us a stack of that day's New York newspapers brought aboard from the Harbor Pilot's boat.

"Please look where the papers are marked," he told us. "Somebody will be joining us soon."

Mary and I went from paper to paper. Every one of them carried a story of the arrival of the "partner of Sherlock Holmes." Most remarked that Dr. Watson and wife simply sought a holiday, but a few speculated that I might be in pursuit of some mystery. The headline of the New York Comet's story appearing just above the fold of the front page proclaimed, "Sherlock Holmes Partner Investigates Wife's Family." That astonishing piece implied my intent to fully investigate the Morstan clan. I must admit I sputtered with outrage.

A new voice came from behind us. "Every newspaper in the city will have reporters at the dock to question you. But we have a plan to avoid that."

Mary and I turned. Behind us stood two men well dressed in American business suits. The one to the rear was tall and thin. As for the one in the lead, robust would be the best description of the fellow. His dark hair was brushed back above his bushy eyebrows. A pair of pince-nez spectacles clung to the bridge of his nose. A slightly shaggy mustache extended a bit past and below the end of his lips. Those lips showed a fair amount of teeth in a grin some might call mischievous.

Somehow I was not surprised when he continued, "Good day, Mrs. Watson. Dr. Watson. I am Theodore Roosevelt."

"Mary and I would be happy if spared this 'honor,' Mr. Roosevelt," I replied.

"Spared you shall be. But, please, call me T.R. as all my friends do. With me is Mr. Robert Van Loan. The Van Loans are old family friends. Though I fear we Roosevelts are johnny-come-latelies to his Dutch clan. It is said that the Van Loans advised the Indians against selling Manhattan Island so that it might become New Amsterdam and later New York.

"As a member of the Federal Civil Service Commission, I have the influence to have you spirited secretly through the Customs inspection. But that would violate the letter and the very spirit of my appointment. Then I remembered that Robert, just this week, has been appointed to head the Customs Service for this region. Few, if any, of those working for him know him by sight. He brought from Washington three of the very best Inspectors of that service. They are to inspect the local inspectors, so to speak. Under the watchful eye of the Third Officer those three are inspecting your luggage at this very moment. Robert here, and his mother's secretary, shall become Doctor and Mrs. John N. Watson. Into the trunks they brought aboard will be hidden many illicit items. Quite a test for those waiting at the docks. Right, Robert?"

"Indeed," said Van Loan, looking as though he felt lucky to have managed to get a word in. "T.R.'s idea. No, it is a scheme really. This bit of drama shall allow me first-hand knowledge of those I will be managing. And you will still make a legal and proper landfall. If my own people fail to arrest me, 'Dr. Watson' shall meet the press to tell them of their 'mistake' in identification."

And so it was. No sooner had the ship docked than Mary and I were spirited off by a Revenue Service cutter from the opposite side of the ship. The cutter dropped us some distance away. Waiting were a small baggage dray and an open-topped carriage.

"A bully fine spring day for an uncovered ride through the city," proclaimed T.R. as he assisted Mary aboard. With the baggage preceding us, the driver took his time along the finest of roads while T.R. pointed out landmarks, parks, and places of historical interest on the way to his family home in the Gramercy Park neighborhood. I must say, Holmes, my first impression of T.R.'s city remained unchanged, even to the day that Mary and I left for home. In many ways New York City is like every other large modern city, but she has about her an energy and pace faster than all others I have visited.

***

The following morning I rose to find the day well advanced as New York is so many hours behind London. My post crossing lethargy was compounded somewhat by T.R.'s seemingly boundless energy and enthusiasm.

"Ah, Watson, there you are," he began as he positively bounced into the room. "Break your fast but lightly. I have a wonderful luncheon planned for us. The women of the household plan to kidnap your good wife for the purpose of showing her off around our circles. The only men present will be those too infirm to escape.

"Meanwhile, you and I will see some of the lesser known by-ways of the city. We shall stop briefly at my office where I shall sign whatever papers await. Then we will proceed to one of the finest places to eat in the city. A place that serves food of a quality rarely seen in an off-the-beaten-path location. After our meal I shall endeavor to show you any attraction of our city you may wish to see."

Shortly we set out with T.R. driving what he referred to as "a simple two-place rig." Soon after we left his immediate neighborhood he turned from the very fine streets of yesterday's route.

"I brought you from the docks only by the best looking streets. With no women with us, nor men given to the vapors, you will see much of the real city, and we shall save a goodly amount of time."

As lost in this large city as I felt the previous day, I became positively bewildered as we wound through secondary streets, alleys, small areas of open ground, and the grounds of various institutions. Wherever we went came frequent calls of greeting to either "Mr. Roosevelt" or "T.R." He cheerfully returned them all, calling many by name. I heard the American version of English accented by many other tongues, and not a few greetings were themselves in other tongues.

It was all too much for me to really absorb in a coherent manner. Still I was reminded of how various trips with one Sherlock Holmes opened my eyes to parts of London I'd never dreamed existed. As we returned to a main thoroughfare I commented on this.

T.R. replied, "This dates to my time on the City Council. I felt compelled to learn more about the people who I represented, and the city in general. I met so many for whom city government was a complete mystery. For many, if not most, I was the first part of the political process they'd ever encountered. Save possibly some self-serving ward-heeler. Nowadays I try to keep up with changes. I still can tell you which areas are simply odd or unusual, and which are actually dangerous."

When we finally stopped all I could have said about our destination was that its location was the island of Manhattan. Now, you well know, Holmes, I am far from fond of lifts, or elevators, as the Americans call them, but T.R.'s office was located in a nine story building. As we rose to the sixth floor I commented on the smoothness of the ride. T.R. asked the operator to explain. This he did saying that Otis Brothers & Company not yet four years ago began producing these "direct-connected geared electric elevator machines." The car in which I rode was among the very first installed.

When we reached the offices of the Civil Service Commission, T.R. proceeded through them like an extremely polite whirlwind. He greeted all he met pleasantly and by name. He received concise reports. Asked incisive questions and received answers while affixing his initials and full signature to various papers and documents. He paused only twice. In the first instance he gave civil, but blunt, instructions for one fellow to stop "beating around the bush" and reach his point. As to the second, he noticed a ring of engagement on one of the young typists' finger. He left her small desk with a full description and history of her intended. I simply followed in his wake the whole time. I concluded that if all government staff operated as did T.R., the world would be a far different place.

As we waited for the elevator, T.R. wrote in a small notebook. "Watson," he said, "though I hold a politically appointed position, I believe in giving the people of our country value for my services. I keep track of all the time I spend in activities related to improving treatment of Federal workers and the quality of work that they do. In some cases I make enemies for my efforts. But I am able to account for all that I do and the Why of it. Ah, here is the car, now."

Instead of returning to the street, T.R. asked the operator to take us up. He then borrowed a key from the chap. A moment later we emerged on the structure's roof, a full ten stories above the ground. The island of Manhattan lay spread out around us. At ten stories few buildings obstructed our view. T.R. pointed out various landmarks.

Once again, in the distance, I saw the statue of Liberty Enlightening The World. From memory my companion recited Emma Lazarus' full sonnet *The New Colossus*. I had read the poem at the time of the statue's erection, but Theodore Roosevelt's emotional recitation of those fourteen lines gave me a larger insight into the character of the United States of America than if academics were to lecture me for a fortnight.

"Watson, do you see that island off to the side of the statue's? I have been spending a bit of time there, and shall be spending quite a bit more in the future. That is Ellis Island. This very year the place becomes the new portal of immigrants for our city and for a large part of our nation."

Back on the streets T.R. again ducked and darted our carriage so that I became hopelessly lost again. "Next we cross Canal Street," he said. "In this area one can find food from all over the world. Most of it is of excellent quality. However, I always inspect the kitchen of any restaurant I patronize, and especially the more expensive ones. Far too often a clean kitchen takes a rear seat to making the dining room look opulent. Surely, as a military man, you must have seen bad food take its toll."

I mentioned to him one or two instances, Holmes, that I have recited to you in detail. Bonaparte had the right of it. An Army travels on its stomach, or may not travel at all when its food is bad.

But, to continue: After we crossed Canal Street, T.R. began to point out small establishments that served food from all parts of the world. I remember him saying Russian Borscht lay in that direction while Nabil of Lebanon served exquisite stuffed grape leaves the opposite way. Along with the sound and odor of factories of the area, I could indeed smell the aromas of a dozen different kitchens.

T.R. tied up his horse near a place with a simple sign saying only "Gio's." He paused to give the animal its feedbag, remarking that the horse had done the real work of the day, thus far.

Then he led me inside saying, "Giovanni Martinelli, our host, is from the north of Italia. He offers a wider selection than his more refined appearing competitors, and his kitchen stays immaculate no matter how busy. Fortunately we have arrived before the crush of workers seeking lunch. Come, I'll introduce you."

The fixtures and furniture inside showed all the signs of heavy use and wear, but the tables and covers could have passed any inspection for cleanliness one could name. As we entered, a group of women—the only other customers—made a cheerful and apparently satisfied exit. Soon we chatted with the proprietor, a robust man of my height and about sixty years. As he explained the restaurant's offerings we heard a most dreadful crash from behind the portal to the kitchen.

Giovanni dashed to the doors of the kitchen. He tried to push through the one opening inward only to find it blocked. T.R. and I reached him as he pulled the other door open. The action caused length of wood some three inches thick by a foot wide to slide to the floor blocking the door open. What we saw put me in mind of a pre-dawn morning in Afghanistan when an earthquake collapsed part of a building where our troops billeted. Now, a very high, long, and deep row of shelving, and its heavy contents, lay in shattered sections covering floor, food preparation tables, and unfortunately several people.

As he took in the scene, Giovanni whispered what I took to be a short prayer in Latin. Then he turned to the boy who had been rolling sets of flatware into napkins at one of the tables. "Antonio," he called out in a steady voice, "get your grandmother! And her bag!"

The lad took off like a shot as I began to look at the injured. I immediately counted five. Others, however, might still be under piles of huge pans and smashed crockery. The eyes of the fellow nearest me moved in their sockets without seeming intention or focus. A small amount of blood came from where a chunk of wood had impacted his scalp. As I snatched up his arm to check his pulse I called out, "See that all the others are not bleeding. Then see if they breathe."

As Giovanni repeated that in Italian I looked around for T.R. To my surprise he stood in the doorway to the street. He removed a metallic object from a pocket. He put this to his lips. By its shrill sound it produced I deduced it to be the local version of the police whistle.

I turned back to see our host and his remaining kitchen staff moving among the debris. My man had a strong pulse, but obviously he was without his wits due to the blow. Then one of the kitchen staff reached a man writhing in pain on the floor. As a wide flat pan was pushed away a large meat grinder came into view, and the arm it had landed on.

"Don't move him!" I cried out. "His arm is broken, badly." For I could see a shard of bone protruding from his sleeve.

A lull in the sounds came briefly over the kitchen. Above the low moaning of the victims I heard the rush of footsteps on the sidewalk outside. I spared a glance to the outer door. The Constable On Patrol must have been very close by, for he dashed up unwinded.

"Sir," he asked T.R., "I trust you have a good reason to use that whistle!"

"See that all the others are not bleeding!"

"We need medical help, Officer," replied T.R. As he began to describe the accident I turned back toward the injured.

In that move my eyes focused on a part of the fallen shelving. Suddenly I felt the bile in my stomach rise. Thanks to you, my good Holmes, I understood what I saw. I swallowed hard, then loudly called out, "T.R.! This is no accident. This was a deliberate crime!"

Before I could say more, one of the kitchen men cried, "He bleed. He bleed!"

Praying that T.R. believed me, and that he could convince the Police Officer, I hurried to the newly uncovered victim. The portly man wore a fresh apron beneath the debris. A crushed chef's hat lay by his head. Someone had lifted a length of the shelf framing off of the man's arm, and he began to bleed profusely. A shard of broken china had been driven into his arm. Blood welled around it. I noticed that the fellow wore braces, as did I.

"A belt," I called out, "or a strap, please!"

At that moment a heavy leather medical bag appeared at my side. Fine female hands yanked open the top to reach in. An instant later I held a dedicated tourniquet, old, but fully ready for use.

I began to apply the device without looking up. I do believe I muttered a word of thanks, but only by reflex. Then a fine contralto voice said, "I'll look to the others, doctor."

I got the tourniquet in place with barely time to spare in terms of lost blood. I slit open the poor man's sleeve with my pen knife. As I began to remove the pottery shard I felt movement beside me. The contralto voice came again.

"One man probably concussed. The compound arm fracture that you have seen. The others seem to have been luckier. Bumps, bruises, minor cuts, and such."

Still intent on the man's arm I replied without looking up. "Thank you, madam...." For I had noticed the wedding ring on her hand as it dove into the miraculously arriving bag.

"I am Maureen, Mrs. Martinelli."

At that moment I reached a point where I could spare her a glance. From almost prone on the floor I looked up, and it seemed like the Goddess Minerva stood over me. This was not the pudgy little Italian woman I might have pictured. Here stood an older woman in a much younger one's body. Her hair, now mostly gray, must have once been a flaming red. Giovanni appeared beside her. I then realized she stood as tall as her husband. A few years younger, Holmes, and she might have posed for Liberty herself.

As soon as I finished with the lacerated blood vessels, Maureen Martinelli offered to finish stitching the wound while I attended the others.

"I take it you have some experience at this, Mrs. Martinelli?" Obviously, she did, but I felt I must inquire.

"I was not out of my teens when I spent the last year of our Civil War working with Clara Barton and her associates. I still do the occasional patching and stitching."

The chef bit down on a heavy leather mouthpiece she produced from her medical bag. Swabbing the wound with alcohol must have hurt terribly. As I prepared to set the other man's arm she talked to the chef, even as she stitched him up like one of Mr. Howe's machines.

Once sure he was not needed to assist with the injured, T.R. appointed himself as gatekeeper to Gio's. He kept the curious out and let family members of the injured in. Finally a man with graying temples and a medical bag entered.

"Good morning, Dr. Adams," called Mrs. Martinelli.

"You've left me but little to do, it seems," he replied.

Dr. Adams and I set that badly broken arm. We then consulted about the other injured men. We made them all as comfortable as possible in the dining room while waiting for transportation to home or hospital.

About that time a well dressed young looking man arrived. I saw him talk briefly to T.R. through the glass of the doors. I felt a bit puzzled until the young fellow called out and the Police Officer summoned by T.R.'s whistle pushed through the gawkers to take my new friend's place at the door. As Dr. Adams and I lashed the now splinted arm in place, T.R. conducted the apparent police detective into the kitchen.

I watched surreptitiously as T.R. showed the man where I had been when I stated that a crime had been committed. He looked around for a moment to take in the entire scene. Then he put himself into the very position I had occupied. He looked toward the door, then back. I thought I saw a gleam in his eye for a brief moment. Then he schooled his face back to a neutral expression. With that he began examining various areas of the huge set of shelves. He made a number of notations in a small book. I believe he drew a few quick sketches, as well. In fact, his actions reminded me no little of you, Holmes.

T.R. and Giovanni answered a number of his questions. Finally he headed in my direction.

"Sir, I am Detective Walter Brooks of the New York City Police. Can you spare the time to show me what made you think this was not an accident?"

At Dr. Adams' nod I rose. I led the way back into the kitchen. I pointed to the same piece that had caught his eye.

"The load bearing portions of these substantial shelves were connected with what we British sometimes call 'tree-nails.' I am not sure what Americans may call them."

"Dowels," interjected T.R, and Brooks nodded.

"This dowel, then, has been weakened by somebody cutting it all round with an extremely fine toothed saw. The center then sheered when an otherwise acceptable strain came on it. I do not doubt that you will find others similarly weakened. In fact, I noticed sawdust at the edge of the back wall."

T.R. spoke up, "But Giovanni uses sawdust as a sweeping agent, as do many restaurants."

"That is true, Detective," said Giovanni.

"I believe I know the variety that you mean," I replied. All the while very glad that I was with you on that case in Nottingham, Holmes. The evidence was quite similar. With that I picked up a scrap of clean bandage that Maureen had cut off and discarded. Using my trusty pen-knife I scraped some of the dust in question onto the cloth.

"That sort of sweeping compound is used in Britain, as well. Or something decidedly similar, I'm sure," I continued. "It is made up of freshly cut pine or other evergreens for the most part. The moisture and pitch pick up dust and dirt. This sawdust, on the other hand, comes from very well cured wood. It has little moisture, and I'm sure a close inspection will show that this is a mixture of pine from the saw blade scraping the main boards and some hardwood like maple from the dowels."

With that I held out the cloth to Detective Brooks. Almost instantly he produced a magnifying lens almost the twin of yours, old friend. It was all I could do not to burst out laughing, so familiar was the action.

"I do see what you mean, Doctor. Doctor...?" he added an inquiring note. I glanced at T.R. who attempted to stifle that mischievous grin. Only then did I realize that he had withheld my name from the eager young detective.

"Watson," I said softly.

I swear, Holmes, that I could nearly see and hear the gears and governors spin and stop in the man's head. A doctor, a British doctor who could identify a felonious situation? When my name took hold his eyebrows shot up.

"Watson? Doctor John H. Watson, formerly of Her Majesty's 5th Northumberland Fusiliers?"

"The same," I replied with a slight smile.

Suddenly my hand was being wrung as if the fellow wanted it for a souvenir.

***

Twenty minutes later Maureen Martinelli prepared an impromptu luncheon for myself, T.R., and Detective Brooks in the family home above the restaurant. Dr. Adams accompanied the seriously injured to a local hospital. Giovanni, and the remaining kitchen staff, waited for a man from the Blackhawk Insurance Company to review the damage before beginning the massive project of putting Gio's back in business.

T.R. asked Brooks, "Who might have perpetrated this unholy incident?"

"I have a fair idea, Mr. Roosevelt," he replied. "However, suspecting and proving are two far different things. I'm sure Dr. Watson is well aware of that. However, I am far ahead of the situation thanks to your friend. Had he not recognized the sabotage for what it was, that lumber would soon have been cut up for salvage and reuse. At that point it becomes useless as evidence. But forewarned, I was able to reach a photographer friend who is now taking pictures of the whole room and close ones of the sabotaged pieces. As he finishes each of those, Officer O'Brien stands by with a good saw to cut off and pack away those pieces as formal evidence. Chances are in a few days somebody would have approached Mr. Martinelli, claimed responsibility, and demanded an extortion payment. So called 'protection' from further incidents. But then again this may not happen. A wise criminal knows when a scheme, or part of one, is beyond salvage.

"It is my hope that mixing New York police procedure with the methods of Mr. Sherlock Holmes will allow me to bring the actual saboteur, and especially his boss, to book. But not soon, I fear."

"I take it, Detective Brooks, that the good Mr. Roosevelt did not use my name in your conversation downstairs."

"No, he did not," replied Brooks with a crooked grin. "He used the term 'my doctor friend.' It is probably just as well that I was not distracted at that point. In spite of some successes, my stated reliance on Mr. Holmes' methods is something of a running joke both on the force, and by newspaper reporters."

"'Some successes' is an understatement, Watson," replied T.R. "Detective

Brooks can be as dogged as an angry badger. Thanks to my City Council time I hear things that many others do not. This case is in good hands."

Later that afternoon T.R. and I emerged from the store called Tiffany's in the five hundredth block of Broadway street. There I had purchased some small items with which to surprise Mary when back in London. We resumed our conversation about Brooks and the police force.

"Simply put, my friend," remarked T.R., "most senior police officials are aware that Sherlock Holmes existed. However, they take your accounts as highly exaggerated. Something akin to the Brothers Grimm in their level of reality. Please do not take offense at my repeating their view. In spite of this, Brooks impresses people. He has every chance to go far. Hopefully more intelligent and imaginative men like him will be attracted to police work. For they are needed, just as the solid beat officer is needed.

"Unfortunately, the investigators of our own popular fiction only reinforce the negative view of your friend. Old Sleuth and Old Cap Collier not only solve mysteries and uncover secrets, but they leave whole platoons of pummeled criminals in their wake. The King Brady team are but little more realistic. Unfortunately your Holmes stories are often tarred with the same brush of disbelief."

"I quite understand, T.R. I encounter some of the same issues in regard to fictional characters in our own so called Penny Dreadfuls. The fictional accounts of the very real Sexton Blake suffer from similar 'enhancement.' Speaking of large reputations, is yonder horseman who I think he might be?"

T.R.'s eyes followed the direction I pointed. Coming our way at an easy walk came a beautiful white horse with riding tack just as outstanding. Astride the horse sat a man in highly adorned fringed bleached buckskin. A hat of the ten gallon variety partially matched the rider's somewhat graying mustache and goatee. A second later a wry chuckle came from my companion.

"Indeed, Watson, that is truly Colonel 'Buffalo Bill' Cody. I did not know he was in town. This must be about his last run of the day."

"Last run?" I inquired. "Whatever do you mean, T.R.?"

"He is on his way to the Beadle and Adams publishing house. It is they who issue the Dime Novels purporting to record his real life adventures. When William is in the city he dresses up in his finest show costume. Then, five or six times a day, he rides his horse to the front door of said publishers. Everyone is supposed to think he has important business to conduct, or new stories to relate. In reality, he soon slips out the back door, then heads for another part of town to make the journey anew. Visitors to the city spread the word, as you might back in London."

With that T.R. stepped from the curb with his arm raised calling, "William! William! William F! Hop down off that equine hulk and meet someone!"

A moment later the renowned Buffalo Bill made an acrobatic dismount from his horse right in front of us. "T.R.," he said as the two shook hands, "good to see you."

"And you, William," replied T.R. with a smile. "I'd like to make you acquainted with Dr. John Watson of London."

As we shook hands Colonel Cody flabbergasted the both of us by saying, "A pleasure, Doctor. In fact as I was conveyed across the city I read about you in the New York Clarion. My congratulations on your saving lives earlier today."

Both T.R. and I stood there open mouthed. Finally I managed to say, "I had no idea the incident would be mentioned by the press."

"My dear sir, when the associate of Sherlock Holmes both saves a life and launches a police investigation, that is indeed news. Reports on this sort of attack on honest businessmen will be the bread and butter of the new owner of the Clarion. Perhaps you have met him out in the Dakotas, T.R., Franklin Havens?"

"Bully!" cried T.R. "I have met him a time or two. The city, and the nation, need more journalists like him. I had not realized it was he who purchased the paper that is now the Clarion."

"You must tell me about this man later, T.R.," I said. "Col. Cody, I am glad for the opportunity to meet you at last. Holmes and I saw your Command Performance in '87."

"Really, Doctor," replied Cody. "I would have enjoyed meeting you and Mr. Holmes, had you come behind the scenes that night."

"We were behind the scenery already, sir. We investigated a totally false threat to Her Majesty, said to be in the mind of one of your performers. We quickly assured ourselves the plot was indeed a fiction. Then, still dressed as dustmen, we stayed for the show. When Her Majesty stood and bowed to your flag I nearly lost my hearing to the screaming of your grooms and stagehands."

"That is not surprising, Dr. Watson," said Buffalo Bill, a far away look in his eyes. "For you saw history made that evening."

"Indeed, Watson," continued T.R. in a very earnest voice. "For the very first time the Stars and Stripes was saluted by a foreign head of state in that ruler's own country. I hope, that act finally finished burying the hatchet, so to speak, between your nation and ours."

After a few more pleasantries we parted ways with Buffalo Bill. As we took yet another short-cut laden route, I took note that the many American flags flying seemed to differ in the area of the blue Union. When I mentioned this T.R. began a storied explanation.

"With each new State added to the Union a new star is added to the flag. I doubt you will observe Old Glory with fewer than thirty-eight stars on your visit. The thirty-eight star flag flew beginning in 1876. So long as flags are fit to fly, they may be used indefinitely. In 1889 we added North and South Dakota, Montana, and the State of Washington, in about ten days. You will see only a few of the forty-two star flags, because we also added Idaho and Wyoming in July of 1890. The newest flags will have forty-four stars. A new flag design was created for each state, but would have been executed but rarely indeed for those intervening numbers.

"Let us look at the flags we pass, Watson. I shall try to identify the number of stars."

Those flags hanging from poles jutting from the sides of buildings T.R. easily identified. Then we approached an intersection with a tiny plot of grass and newly emerged spring flowers at its center. From the midst of the greenery sprang a twenty foot pole topped by a sizable American flag drifting only slightly in the light breeze.

T.R. changed to the center lane of traffic so that we might pass close by, saying, "This will be a bit of a challenge, my friend. Let me look... *Hold on Watson!*"

As T.R. spoke, a strong puff of wind threw the flag hard away from the pole. Somehow the halyard parted. The large flag weighted by rope, grommets, and clips quickly fluttered down directly in front of our carriage. As he cried that warning T.R. rose from his seat to haul back on the reins as hard as he could. I grabbed the side rail and the front of the rig as hard as *I* could. For the horse reared up like a Lipizzaner stallion in a show.

T.R. vaulted out of the carriage just as soon as he managed to set the brake. He calmed the horse for an instant or two before moving ahead to where the Stars and Stripes lay on the dusty pavement. After but the briefest of looks at the fallen colors he snatched them from the ground with all the fervor of a man yanking a relative about to go over a cliff.

He held the bundle carefully in his arms for a second. Then he turned his gaze to me as I joined him in front of the still nervous horse.

"Watson," he said in an almost pleading tone as he removed the clips from the grommets, "I know these colors are not the ones you acknowledge, but would you please bear me a hand?"

"Of course, my friend. How may I help?"

"Please take the corners of the end with the blue Union. Now we will pull everything taut. Fine. Now let us turn the colors over. Excellent, Old Glory only picked up a bit of dust. That she can shake out when she flies proudly again. Were there stains or tears the flag would have to be destroyed.

"Let us shake her a bit to remove what dust we can. Now we fold the stripes over the Union. Next fold in half again so that the blue is visible top and bottom. Very good. Keep your end taut at all times and step toward me as I begin to fold."

With that, T.R. began folding the stripes of the flag into an isosceles right-triangle. He continued folding as I approached him. About half way through the procedure a Police Officer came hurrying up. I suppose he wanted to know why our carriage blocked part of a busy pair of streets. I nearly dropped my end of the flag when he realized what we were doing. With a last step he sprang to attention and crisply saluted until we had finished. In addition, three carriages and a heavy beer wagon halted, with some of the drivers standing. A truly astonishing sight, Holmes.

As he stuffed the remaining material neatly inside the triangular bundle T.R. remarked, "Three sided, Watson, for the tri-cornered hat of 1776. Excuse me, Officer...?"

"Jablonsky, sir!"

"Jablonsky, do you know who should take charge of this flag until yonder halyard can be repaired?"

"Yes, indeed, sir."

"Then may I ask you to deliver Old Glory to that person?"

"Of course, sir!"

We then headed back to T.R.'s home without further incident. But, Holmes, I'll be jiggered, we received a small round of applause for our efforts as we boarded our carriage.

"A most interesting incident, Watson," remarked Holmes as he refreshed our coffee cups from the sideboard. "I have known that many Americans seem far more serious about their flag than most peoples. Perhaps you can tell me the 'why' of it."

"I discussed this with T.R. on several occasions as we traveled. The best point I can put forward is that the flag is their common history and common heritage as Americans. That Officer, Jablonsky, may have been born in the United States, but perhaps not his parents. Giovanni, the Italian restaurateur, married to an Irish colleen and not to another Italian. But they are Americans all.

"T.R. told me he once met an Englishman who had written a book about all flags of the world. The man concluded that Americans lavished so much care and ceremony on their flag because they lack a Royal Family to heap honors upon. My friend was definitely not amused by that idea.

"At this point, Holmes, I shall take a liberty with my narrative that I do not when recounting your cases...."

These things I learned much later, and mostly from Detective Brooks. T.R. had the right of it. The young man was indeed both intelligent and dogged. He suspected an ex-patriot Englishman who used the nom-de-criminal of "The Gentleman Dodger."

Holmes' bark of laughter broke into my narrative.

"Ha! Dickens must be restless in his grave at that!"

"That I do not doubt, Holmes," I replied, "but the man himself was serious as the grave indeed." Then I continued.

Detective Brooks, with the story from the New York Clarion fresh in the ears of his superiors, had little trouble requisitioning the official help he wanted. A close but discrete watch went out on the Dodger. And a retired officer of great strength and patience secretly established himself in the attic of the small carriage house at the rear of the Roosevelt home.

At his office late that evening the Dodger received an unknown visitor. How the watching police managed to hear some of the conversation I do not know. Whatever the method, they were astonished by what little they heard and deduced. The Dodger had come to know the so-called etiquette of New York crime. He carved out a territory of his own, but did not invite conflict with other bosses. When conflict did come, however, he was said to fear no one.

The Dodger's visitor came with the proper introductions and words to warrant a private interview. He spoke with a false Scottish brogue that the watchers believed rode atop a refined English voice. When the initial small talk ended the two spoke in tones too low to be understood. But one thing became certain, the Gentleman Dodger, more than ten years one of New

York's ablest and most independent criminal bosses, began to take orders from this visitor.

***

The Watsons and the Roosevelts spent the next two days in social activities and planning the course of seeking Mary's possible relatives. What we did not understand was that our quest had long since attracted unwanted attention.

Well it was that T.R. had used Mr. Legengre's firm and the mail to reach me. For as it turned out the transatlantic cables were rigged against us in a manner that frightened even your brother Mycroft. It seems that one major stockholder in the cable companies held an interest, though most would deem it an obsession, with the name Morstan. His lack of scruples must be nigh on the same as Professor Moriarty's. This man, under various names and companies, personally held, or controlled, large blocks of stock in every overseas cable company.

Thus he placed men of his own organization in all the major hubs of communication in Great Britain and many other places. These men and some devilish devices based on the common stock ticker-tape machine scoured the supposedly confidential traffic of information under the seas. Only strongly coded messages escaped their full scrutiny.

The underlings received lists of words and combinations of words to find as they scanned the daily traffic from seemingly all the world. Most had to do with companies and governments. Some few covered movement of pieces of fine arts, and a certain small number meant nothing at all to the searchers. One such word, from the very beginning, had been Morstan. After Mary and I wed, my name and yours, Holmes, were added. With special attention to be paid to our messages to the Americas. The word Morstan never appeared in telegraph messages between T.R. and myself. However the term "Mary's family" did, and that soon reached the puppeteer manipulating all those strings.

No real information of our plans could be deduced, other than that we intended to travel outside the City of New York. But that was enough that watches were initiated on all likely venues where T.R., or members of his family or staff, might book transportation beyond the five Burroughs of New York.

When T.R. arranged for train tickets to the Adirondacks several things happened: Messages flew back and forth across the Atlantic; requests, really commands, for men of certain skills went to the Dodger; and T.R.

and the Watsons, nearly worry free, packed lightly for a trip to the town of Warrensburg, in the State of New York's Adirondack mountain area.

The following morning we boarded the train for the trip of about seven hours total. As you know, Holmes, most American train cars are not compartmented as they are in Europe. Indeed they are more like the train cars for the natives I saw in India. Fortunately T.R. managed to secure us a Pullman car compartment. Our staying in that closed-off area may have postponed some of the planned mischief against us.

T.R. kept us entertained like a professional tour guide until we reached the rural areas. Some fields were being worked to plant spring crops, but a heavy rain the day before kept the farmers out of the fields that day. The greening land soon became a blur of sameness.

As Mary studied the just published "Death-bed Edition" of Whitman's Leaves of Grass, I cast about for something to do. (Writing story notes on a train usually gives me a loathsome headache.)

"This," said T.R. looking up with a crooked smile from a volume of on European history, "is why I always pack much to read for a railroad journey. Otherwise, save for small town papers only of interest to small townspeople, you must make do with such as this."

With that he handed me a pamphlet much like one of our notorious Penny Dreadful story papers. Marked as by Buffalo Bill's own publishing house, the masthead read:

Beadle's Half-Dime Library, Beadle and Adams Publishers, No. 98
William Street, New York. Price, 5 Cents.

DEADWOOD DICK

THE PRINCE OF THE ROAD;
or,
THE BLACK RIDER OF THE BLACK HILLS.

by Edward L. Wheeler.

After a few pages the protagonist was described as follows:

His form was clothed in a tight-fitting habit of buck-skin, which was colored a jetty black, and presented a striking contrast to anything one sees as a garment in the wild far West. And this was not all, either. A broad black hat was slouched down over his eyes; he wore a thick black veil over the upper portion of his face, through the eye-holes of which there gleamed a pair of orbs of piercing intensity, and his hands, large and knotted, were hidden in a pair of kid gloves of a light color.

The "Black Rider" he might have been justly termed, for his thoroughbred steed was as black as coal, but we have not seen fit to call him such—his name is Deadwood Dick, and let that suffice for the present.

"I first read the tale while at Harvard. It is often reprinted," T.R. said with a slightly wistful tone as I looked up, "and there must be nigh on a hundred more in the sequence. There actually was, and maybe still is, someone calling himself Deadwood Dick. Those writings about him are outrageous beyond reason. Still the man's, or men's, reputation built itself on standing up for the downtrodden. A bit of your Robin Hood, so to speak."

"This very year," commented T.R. as our train began a long uphill grade, "some six-and-one-tenth million acres of land became the Adirondack Park. Nearly one half is owned by the State of New York. The rest of these mountains are in private hands, but what can be done on that land is now heavily controlled. No logging or mining allowed.

"Of course, the timber barons and the mining interests are appalled. In the minds of most of them their right to mindlessly destroy wilderness and God's Creations in general is self-evident. They see the beauty created by the Almighty as nothing compared to the luster of the dollar. With the ink of that new law not yet dry, their minions are arm-twisting and probably blackmailing every member of our State Legislature they can reach."

He paused to wipe the sheen of perspiration from his forehead. Reaching inside his valise he extracted a sheaf of papers. "Excuse me orating like a stump speaker, my friends, but the matter of preserving the wonders of nature is very dear to my heart. Left alone, the barons will chip away at the Adirondack Park until it means nothing. Ah, here it is. The Roosevelts will be backing a newly proposed amendment to the State Constitution. I believe a solid vote of the people will block the rascals for good, and all. The draft of the ballot measure reads, 'The lands of the state, now owned or hereafter acquired, constituting the forest preserve as now fixed by law, shall be forever kept as wild forest lands. They shall not be leased, sold or exchanged, or be taken by any corporation, public or private, nor shall the timber thereon be sold, removed or destroyed.' With this passed and in place, naught but an armed revolution can overturn it.

"What the two of you see in the region of our destination will be much the same when our many times great-grandchildren visit."

***

Our journey required that we change trains more that once. Finally we reached the modest sized town of Saratoga Springs. With but little difficulty we changed to the local Adirondack Railway. T.R. explained that the small rail line existed only to serve the large number of hotels in the region. When we reached the end-of-tracks we would continue by stage coach.

"We journey about 25 miles by road to the town called Warrensburg," remarked T.R. "Hereabouts the roads are generally well maintained. The local hotels and so-called 'Great Camps' wish for return business, rather than to lose customers to those closer to the cities."

The weather that afternoon turned briskly cool, but with a brilliant spring sun. After all, T.R. informed us we were at over fifteen-hundred feet of altitude. By mutual consent we, meaning the three of us and two locals returning home, kept the isinglass windows of the comfortable coach partly open as the sunlight heated our laps enough that light wraps sufficed to keep all comfortable. Again, T.R. had the right of it: The roads we traversed were indeed in fine condition.

We made excellent time, at least by English standards. With leaves yet sparse on the trees we had some amazing views of the mountains thereabouts. For a time we paralleled a stream one of the locals told us was the North River. About halfway to Warrensburg we crested one of the many hills on the roadway. Just on the downslope the driver brought the four horse carriage to a stop.

"One of my horses needs attention," called the driver from his perch. "You folks kin get out and look around, if you like. I hain't left a body behind, ever. Jus' don't stray too far."

The local folks settled deeper into their seats, but the three of us soon exited the coach to see the sights. In another three or four weeks much of what we could see would become invisible as the forest finished producing the new season's leaves. Mary extracted a pair of good opera glasses from her handbag. As she scanned the riverbed below, T.R. stretched his arms as he walked back to the crest of the hill. As Mary enjoyed the view I reveled in the cool fresh air. Then I glanced after T.R.

As my gaze fell on him, my friend ducked down. He came back toward the coach somewhat crouched over. Reaching me he resumed his usual ramrod straight stance. A moment later he borrowed Mary's opera glasses and headed back to the crest beckoning me to follow.

Follow I did, but not directly to the crest. T.R. eased himself past the edge of the road's gravel and into the large trees along its border. After all the times I'd followed one Sherlock Holmes into unusual situations I kept behind my new friend as he picked his way through moss and last year's leaves.

Just over the hill's crest T.R. looked out from behind a huge oak tree. Putting Mary's glass to his eyes, he struggled with the focus because of his pince-nez spectacles. At last he muttered, "Yes, yes. There he is."

"There is whom?" I asked in a whisper.

"A horseman of dubious intent, Watson. When I crested this hill he followed the road at about the same rate as our coach. I could barely see him for the hill between us. But my guess is that he caught sight of the top of the coach which is much taller than I. He brought his steed to a halt, then moved off into the trees. Most any honest man would have continued on his way, or stopped by the coach to offer assistance. He did neither. I ducked out of sight before he got sight of me, I am fairly sure. I fear this fellow's up to no good."

"Could he be some Officer of the Law watching over the coach?" I asked.

"A possibility, I admit, however remote. But were there 'highwaymen,' to use the English term, about this area, I feel I would have heard of it. I could not get a very good look at his face. However, he carries something strapped across his back that I fear might be a rifle case."

"Please do not worry Mary at this time, T.R.," I asked as we returned towards the coach.

"As you wish," he replied, "but we must keep a sharp watch around us. Perhaps the rider has a score to settle with one of the locals on board, or a debt to collect. Your narrative indicates that Mary is not given to hysteria, nor 'the vapors.' Is this true in real life, as well?"

"Mary is as steady a hand as one can wish for in someone not trained for adventure or danger, my friend."

"Capital!" whispered T.R. as we reached the coach to find Mary holding the left lead horse's bridle. She patted the creature's head and spoke comforting words as the driver tended to one of the creature's hooves.

"A stone jammed in the shoe, sir?" asked T.R.

"Aye," came the reply. "Saw her shy just as i' happened. Not goin' ta pull her out of harness. We'll go a bit slow a while, then see."

"I am grateful for your vigilance. I once walked twenty miles in the far west when the thing happened to my mount."

"'S what they pay me for, sor. But thank you. And thank you, Mrs. Watson, for steadying her. Best be boarding now."

I escorted Mary and handed her up into the coach. Before I pulled myself in, I heard T.R. ask, "Did you know a single rider followed us?"

"Saw him a time or two. Thought he'd be passing by."

"No," replied T.R. in a whisper I could just barely hear. "He hid in the trees."

The coachman muttered something. I do not doubt the words were quite lurid for T.R. grimaced a bit. Again T.R. whispered, "May I ride up top with you? I have a rifle in that bag of golf clubs lashed just behind you."

Few deny Theodore Roosevelt possesses the trait of instilling faith in his honesty in all he meets. Even on our short acquaintance I did not doubt that the driver would agree. As I took my place beside Mary, T.R. called out for all to hear, "My friends, our driver has granted me the favor of sharing his excellent view for the remainder of our journey."

So off we went. The coach arrived only ten minutes past its scheduled time. In that time two noteworthy incidents occurred. First, at about half the remaining distance to Warrensburg, I heard hoofbeats approaching from the rear. I wished I had retrieved my service revolver from my valise in the coach's boot, but nothing untoward happened. Two riders swept past us at a fast, but not nearly breakneck, pace. Each wore a business suit common to well paid New York office workers. Each had a fair sized carpet bag lashed to the rear of his saddle, and one of them carried a long and thin case strapped to his back.

Then, less than a quarter mile from our destination, another road joined into ours from down hill. In the coach I happened to have just the proper angle to see a heavy wagon slow to barely moving in order for our coach to pass. Our somewhat dour driver called a cheery word of thanks as we went by. Beneath the large hat of the other driver I made out a huge grin. Obviously the two men knew each other well. I thought no more about the incident.

No more than three minutes later the coach halted at a large rambling building of three stories. American flags flew at each end of a large sign on the second floor balcony proclaiming "Camp Liberty." A smaller sign,

"Mary is as steady a hand as one can wish for in someone not trained for adventure or danger, my friend."

near ground level, suggested that newly arriving guests proceed to a door to the right, while passers-by were welcome in the Green Mountain Boys' Cafe to the left.

The three of us alighted. As we stretched stiff joints, our two local companions offered pleasant good-byes and headed to the stable across the street to pick up their mounts. In addition several horses were tied to hitching posts outside the facility. Among them I was sure I identified one of the mounts that passed us back on the road.

A moment later our bags adorned the sidewalk near the lobby door. A well groomed young man stood by the luggage with a cart as we entered. We paused briefly just inside. In spite of large and lightly curtained windows, and lamps at the hotel counter, the large room seemed like a tomb after the brightest of spring daylight.

The scene, Holmes, was universal to decent hotels the world over. Chairs and couches with people reading and chatting. Behind the counter a man in his twenties sorted the mail delivery from our coach. Another fellow, a bit older, wrote in a ledger. In the background a woman whose age I took to be about fifty spoke with a very young woman in a maid's uniform. Both women glanced at us as we stood there. The girl barely took us in, but I felt that her superior carefully analyzed our party in that brief moment.

Just before we could begin to move forward, the older man wiped his pen and put it away. He seemed to know exactly how long most people took to adjust to the lower light. With a smile that seemed genuine he said, "Good afternoon, travelers. Welcome to Camp Liberty. How may we help you?"

"And good afternoon to you, sir," replied T.R. stepping forward. "We would like to engage two rooms."

As he neared the counter, the older woman put on a pair of spectacles. She took them off a moment later. Her expression did not change, but she spoke softly to the maid who quickly stepped out of sight. At that I realized that this must be "Mrs. G.," whom T.R's agent mentioned as the probable head of the local Morstan family. Certain I was, also, that she had, in some manner, recognized Theodore Roosevelt.

Barely had T.R. and the other begin to transact business when we heard boots pounding on the sidewalk outside. A young man in his late teens practically pulled the front doors from their hinges entering.

"Fire!" he yelled. "Fire in our quarters!"

***

What we did not know then, Holmes, was that much of Camp Liberty's staff consisted of the extended Morstan family, and that many of them lived in a large building not far behind the one we stood in. Both Mrs. G., for that's who she indeed was, and the older man began to give orders to others in a measured and deliberate fashion some Army Sergeants I have known would have envied.

The guests were instructed to stand fast. The employees urged to assigned duties. All save Mrs. G. vanished on flying feet. Mrs. G. quickly collected ledgers and a cash drawer and took them out of sight. A moment later came the unmistakable sound of a hard closed safe door. Then she hurried out the front door calling across the street asking for assistance from the stable.

As I drew breath to reassure Mary, T.R. said to me, "Watson, can you ride a horse?"

I sputtered an affirmative, but I had no idea what might be on his mind.

"Mary, please stay here, your husband and I go to help."

With that, T.R. almost dragged me out the door and across the street.

We nearly sprinted into the stable. Inside only one old man remained, making sure the horses did not panic should smoke reach the area.

"Sir," cried T.R., "we need a saddled mount now to help with the fire."

With two complete strangers demanding a horse in the middle of an emergency I felt no surprise when the fellow hesitated. I saw T.R.'s finger slip into a coin pocket in the waistband of his trousers. An instant later an American coin I had never before seen appeared on top of a feed bin between us. I later learned the thing was a fifty dollar gold piece. The old man's eye's popped open.

"That is our deposit, sir. Now please show us a mount."

A moment later we stood next to a solid appearing animal of brown and white. Unfamiliar with American tack, I fumbled my mount. T.R. practically threw me into the saddle.

As he took the few seconds necessary to see me properly aboard he informed me, "Go back the way we came. That big wagon we passed carries water. And a pump. Hurry, Watson!"

Later we learned that the old man kept his wits about him. The Paint horse, known as Ethan Allen, served to carry visitors of all levels of skill, or lack of it. But the creature was not afraid to hurry, as I soon found out.

He started out at a fast walk as I urged him to greater speed. I suppose he soon realized I was not going to fall off his back. Our speed increased in successive short stages until I leaned over his neck and clung on to the reins at a fair gallop.

Down the road we flew like an arrow, and I'm not ashamed to admit I remembered a few long forgotten prayers along the way. I have no idea how long the journey took. However, we soon caught up with the slow wagon.

The driver looked back as I came within about fifty yards. I'm sure he thought me demented. He began to move his team to the side of the road. The better, he thought, to avoid the lunatic from the city.

"Stop! Please stop!" I yelled as I began to rein in Ethan Allen. I was thankful that the good horse stopped smoothly. As I came alongside the wagon I called, "Fire at Camp Liberty. In the staff quarters, whereever that is. Please turn back."

The fellow's mouth went grim under his large flat-brimmed hat. "Thank ye, pilgrim. Now head General Allen back there so's I can turn. Now move!"

Move I did. A good furlong back toward Camp Liberty, Ethan Allen and I paused to look back. Now I know how London draymen and teamsters can twist and turn their teams in our streets and allies. What Brother Thaddeus Radcliffe did to turn that team of eight and the huge wagon on a narrow road with a steep downslope to one side I can not begin to describe. I've even tried drawing diagrams of the act a dozen times. In a time seemingly requiring Divine Intervention, the water wagon raced for Camp Liberty at a rate I would not have believed possible save I saw the event with my own eyes.

Once sure of the water wagon's return, I urged my mount back to the Camp. Now knowing my ability to stay aboard, Ethan Allen quickly reached his previous high rate of speed. We fairly flew along the fine graveled road.

Just before I could pull back on the reins, General Allen eased us to a smooth stop at the hitching rail of his home stable. Stopped, I nearly went end over end as I began to dismount. On solid ground once more, I flipped the reins over the painted metal rail and dashed back across the street.

Most, if not all, of the guests were gathered in front of the office doors. Wisps of smoke drifted from around back somewhere. A man of middle age with a pronounced limp wearing Camp Liberty livery watched over the guests, and I found no surprise in seeing the actions of two others. Mary, long a professional governess, gathered some smaller children round her trying to keep their minds off of the crisis. On the other side of the group, T.R. organized the able bodied men to be ready to help the staff if the need arose.

"Success, Watson?" called T.R. as I approached.

"He comes." I gasped as the strain and excitement of the run caught up with me.

"Man of the Camp!" bellowed T.R. at the guests' shepherd. "Brother Radcliffe's water wagon will be here in moments to assist."

The man's expression changed from barely contained worry to great relief. "Thank you, sir," he called back. "I'll direct him. Please keep out of his way." With that he limped hurriedly to the far side of the building.

Immediately T.R. turned his improvised command over to a large man who looked awkward in a business suit. He beckoned to me to follow him to see if help was truly needed.

Obviously Camp Liberty planned extensively in advance for emergencies. We raced past the central building containing the hostelry offices and most of the traditional guest rooms. Further from the road—and separated by a few rows of trees and shrubs—lay another substantial three story building. This we later learned served as the true home of many of the staff, and home away from home for partial-time and summer seasonal employees. Thick dark smoke billowed from the rear of this building. A gust of wind pushed a large patch of it down onto us as we ran. Suddenly I felt stricken like in a London pea-souper, or worse. We both began coughing.

We rounded the second building and out of that noxious cloud taking care not to get in the way of the firefighting efforts. Little flame was visible on the outer wall. More than a dozen exhausted extinguishers of the acid and bicarbonate of soda variety lay scattered on the ground.

Two bucket chains hauled water from rain barrels to be thrown on that outer wall. Other buckets were carried inside. A moment later a man appeared at a third story window to dash a bucket full of water on the wall. Other groups carried trunks, furniture, and such out of distant doors. And well they should, for by smoke seeping out from many places and a muffled crackling sound, I could tell that the flames had entered the interior of the wall.

At that point two men emerged from the trees, staggering with a heavy wooden toolbox between them. Before the thing fully settled on the carpet of leaves outside the crushed rock walkways, the two yanked open the lid. Quickly producing wrecking bars, they ran to the charred wall to rip off the smoldering shingles. Fire flared, then water flew from buckets. And the two attacked the wall again.

Standing behind the organized chaos, the older woman from the Camp's lobby watched. She called encouragement and general directions. A moment later we trotted up to her. By this time I had trouble catching my breath.

"Madam," coughed T.R., "My friend has diverted Brother Radcliffe's water wagon to the Camp. He should be here very shortly."

Her eyes never left the threatened building, but the lines upon her face eased. "Praise the Lord! And thank you, gentlemen. Nathan! See that the way is cleared for the water wagon's approach!"

A sturdy fellow with a huge handlebar mustache handed his bucket to another and dashed off.

T.R. continued, "In addition, I have twenty able-bodied guests ready to volunteer their assistance."

"Thank you, Mr. Roosevelt. If Brother Radcliffe is indeed close we shall not need their help. You and Dr. Watson please stand away so I may concentrate."

We stepped over to an isolated alcove in the bushes and trees but with a good view of the activities. In the distance we could now hear the cracking of a bullwhip and shouts in Brother Radcliffe's unusual version of English.

"T.R., she knows who we are..." I began, but got no further. T.R. began to gasp. And cough, and wheeze. I barely got him seated on the bench in the wooded alcove as his legs began to give way.

T.R.'s face reddened. His mouth moved into a contorted grimacing smile. I heard his labored breathing whistle around his teeth. Then his lips moved with his exhalation. I barely made out the words, "Damned asthma!"

My thoughts were already in that direction when he spoke. Now I could be sure. To see such a vital man struck low by this insidious condition drove home for me once again both the progress and its lack in the medical profession. This was one time that your absence, Holmes, benefited me. For in that period I read much more extensively in the medical journals in English, and even assaying the occasional one in French, than in previous years.

I poked my head outside of the inset in the trees and bushes. Over to the side stood several boys in a loose row. Too small for heavy work, they watched the firefighting efforts with frequent glances at the woman in charge. Runners I immediately took them for. I hurried over and hunched down to be at their eye level.

"Lads," I began, "I need your help. I am a doctor. My friend is having trouble breathing. To treat him I need tea leaves. Will one of you go to the kitchen or dining room? If you can find freshly brewed leaves in a pot that would be the best. If not, a spoonful or two of the dry leaves and some water will do."

The boys looked at each other for a second. Then the one who appeared oldest gestured at the two of the others. They set off at a run.

"Bobby helps out in the kitchen, sir," said the older boy. "He'll know where to look."

I tendered my thanks and returned to T.R. His breathing seemed slightly eased, but far, far, from normal. With agonizing slowness he pulled a flat tin pill box from his coat pocket. "Open this, Watson. The odor seems to sometimes help."

Sealed with wax, the thing gave me a bit of trouble. Then the smell of Eucalyptus leaves hit my face like a barber's hot wet towel. I crushed a couple of leaves and allowed him to breathe in the fumes. Knowing all the while that this was akin to putting a mustard plaster on a bullet wound. Still, he relaxed a bit more; what in medicine is called placebo, I suspect.

A minute later the two boys rushed up. One carried a lacquered metal pitcher of very cold water and a drinking glass. The other juggled a large china teapot, a long spoon, and a metal tin marked "Darjeeling." Thanking the boys, I set about draining and scooping out the steeped leaves from the teapot. From the tin I mixed in some of the dry tea.

"T.R.," I said in my most professional voice, "I want you to put these tea leaves under your tongue. Suck the liquid out of them. Drink some water, if you feel up to it, but keep sucking on those leaves."

With a pained, but curious, look on his face, he complied.

"About four years ago doctors began giving something called theophylline for asthma," I told him. "The chemical is derived from tea leaves. I have no idea just how the derivation process is done, but this surely can not hurt you. The effect of theophylline is to widen the openings of the air passages constricted by your attack."

With that I joined him on the bench. Between breaths T.R. began to work his jaw like a confirmed chewer of tobacco. Hardly a minute went by before we began to see the firefighters give way to the eight horses of the water wagon's team. Soon Brother Radcliffe came into view, calling thanks to the horses as he brought them to a halt. Then with a field drill sergeant's voice he began giving orders to the assembled staff for the deployment of hoses and pump. Not two minutes after that, water rushed out of two hoses as even more men wielded tools to uncover pockets of flame.

Perhaps seeing the situation come under apparent control helped T.R. relax. For soon his breathing eased to nearly normal. A few minutes later he spat out the mass of tea leaves remarking his mouth felt like tanned leather. Soon, using both our coats for a pillow, I allowed him to lay upon the bench. In moments he slept with a normal sounding breathing cycle.

***

About an hour after sunset, Mary and I sat together at a table in the sitting room of our Camp Liberty accommodations. My wife still worked at grasping the meaning of Mr. Whitman's poems, especially the one titled "Passage To India." I, too enjoyed comparing his ideas to Mary's and my own experiences in such a trip. In between her questions and comments I worked writing up my notes on our extremely eventful trip, thus far.

Through the cracked open door connecting to the next room we heard movement. Then came a muffled expression of consternation. Barely above a whisper came the call, "Watson?"

Mary laughed softly as I called out, "In here, T.R."

Bare feet shuffled across the floor. Then our companion's bedraggled head poked around the door blinking in the lamp light. That head withdrew and sounds of a man adjusting slept-in attire reached us. A moment later, except for his tousled hair and bare feet, a sartorially correct Theodore Roosevelt joined us.

Standing before us, he said, "I take it we are within Camp Liberty?"

"Indeed we are, my friend," I replied. "And, as saviors of the day, we inhabit one of the best suites in the facility. This early in the season, they are far from full."

"I remember lying down on that bench. Then seeing the sweet face of a young woman. Now I wake in a fine bed. Please do enlighten me, Watson."

"With the fire under control, Mrs. Gordon (Mrs. G., as she is known) had you brought here on a stretcher. The sweet face was her grandniece, Rebecca, who looks after the sick and injured between visits from a doctor. Well trained and knowledgeable she is indeed. We did not attempt to remove your jacket for fear of waking you. For you surely needed the sleep."

"Indeed. Those vile attacks leave me as limp as a well used washcloth," he replied with disgust. "And were you able to discover how Mrs. Gordon knew who we were?"

"Actually, it was you she identified. Given that she reads most New York papers within twenty-four hours of publication, deducing that Mary and I were your companions was, shall we say, elementary."

T.R. grimaced at the use of one of your favorite words, Holmes. Then he continued, "But how did she know me?"

"It seems that you neglected to learn all there is to know about Mr. Ashley Morstan. He wrote to his mother, Mrs. G.'s daughter-in-law, about your meeting in South Dakota. With his letter he included this striking drawing of you. The likeness is quite good."

"Elementary all around it seems, Watson. Sometimes mysteries are hardly mysteries at all. I hope that the blazing building was saved in the end."

I paused a moment before telling him, "There is a triple fire watch this night, in case an ember was missed. In a week, or less, the structure will be whole again. I am sorry to say that there are also armed patrols in the compound this night. For a man in city dress dashed from the area of the staff quarters just before the fire revealed itself. The three of us are to meet with Mrs. G. for breakfast to discuss Morstan family history and what we might know about these other matters."

We slept the night in comfort. We arose not long after the sun, with T.R. fully re-energized. He told us that cattle driving cowboys referred to our lack of immediate activity as "Burnin' Daylight." In their business a precious commodity.

Shortly after we began moving around, the staff brought in a fine breakfast. Some translation was required into the Queen's English. Neither Mary nor I being familiar with the term "flap-jack," for instance.

At the end of the meal, Mary sipped a cup of Gunpowder tea as only an old India hand might. T.R. and I enjoyed a robust coffee, instead. Soon after, Mrs. G. entered.

After very brief pleasantries she began a convoluted and lengthy narrative on the circumstances which disconnected parts of the Morstan family. The story that brought my Mary to those very rooms.

Mrs. G.'s narrative:

I was about ten years when this began. I had a brother both elder and younger. Sorry I am that the Morstan family, in those days, never felt it necessary to confide problems or important things to their womenfolk. We lived three counties away from Mary's father's branch of the family. I believe that Mary and I are second cousins. The county we lived in was under the control of four very well-to-do landed families.

We were tenants to one of them. From what I did hear from my father and elder brother those families yearned to live, and rule, before the Magna Carta. They considered us chattel. Serfs, and less. Them, and their ruffian overseers, made sure everybody stayed in debt to their masters. Any who considered to move out got threatened with Debtor's Prison, or worse. My father's left arm didn't work quite right from a beating they once gave him.

Then one day daddy came a'rushing home. "I've done it," he cried with joy. "I've done it. We have our freedom."

With that we were told to pack for Australia. My mother 'bout had a fit. I watched from across the room as father related a story to her. All color left her face. I even caught a glimpse of what I now know to be a purse of gold coins and bank notes. Then my mother began to hurry us along packing.

Before evening we departed for Bristol and a ship set to sail to the other side of the world. Father hired a large wagon to haul ourselves and our furniture to the Bristol docks. At the dock I watched as he spoke to the master of the Australia-bound ship. Our furniture disappeared into the ship's hold. With a small cart to hold our "cabin baggage," we departed that dock to purchase provisions for the trip that began the next day.

We walked to a church some distance from the ships and yards. Father convinced the Sexton to let us wait to sail in the church's stables. Once the family settled in, father disappeared out the back door. He returned in haste a few hours later.

Quieter than a band of thieves we snuck out of that same back door. By a roundabout way we returned to another part of the docks. We were hustled aboard another ship in pitch darkness. Almost as soon as we settled below decks the ship cast off her lines. A steam tug, equipped with limelights I discovered later, pulled us out of the harbor to the sea lanes. We came on deck after dawn to find no land in sight. We soon noticed that the crew spoke English unlike any we ever heard before. The reason soon became clear as the Stars and Stripes rose on its halyard. I barely knew that America existed, yet I was on the way to meet her.

To this day I do not know how father found that particular ship nor how he got us admitted into this nation. We came ashore in Portsmouth, New Hampshire. Based on something our father learned from the ship's officers, we made our way west until the Adirondacks rose before us. Not too far from Warrensburg he bought some land and what was needed to survive and build our new home. That, I gather, was when that pouch of money ran out.

We all worked and worked for months. We built the first house our family ever owned. We worked for other people when they needed help. But father insisted that we live at home, so none held sway over us. And so it went for some years.

Then my elder brother married. We had what they call here a "house raising" for him and his bride on the family land. And soon they were blessed with a son. Then another. And I met Mr. Ronald Gordon, the mighty blacksmith hereabouts. And the tenderest of men in his heart. Over ten years older than I, we soon loved each other. Most of his family headed west over the years. Finally, we lived in the largest of his family's homes with room upon room to spare. When visitors began showing up in the area, we started to board them. Before my Ronald passed to his reward we began Camp Liberty.

Not all was well and good, of course. Came the Civil War both my brothers joined the Federalized Militia. Close as we'd been to slavery, there was no stoppin' them. And my younger brother not two months married when he left. He died in battle before his son came into the world. My older brother perished near the end of the war. Ronald and I became the center of the family as my father aged. And catering to visitors became our living.

All might seem perfect to an outsider. We grew and prospered. We are beholden to not a living soul. We have many friends. Our preacher says we've Life, Liberty, and pretty much ended the Pursuit of Happiness. What more could we need?

Others sometimes wonder why we call the place Camp Liberty, 'stead of Morstan's Rest, or some such. Reason is, I'm scared of our name becoming too well known. Father feared us being found by those landed gentry till the day he died.

Sometimes father drank a bit too much. When he did he often became afraid of us being found. "I saw the deed," he'd say. "Saw him run away." Other times he said, "Wrote it out for me, he did. Signed it, in blood. His blood."

In his last years he sealed some papers in an envelope. He had me put them in a safe place. After that when he'd drink he would say things like, "If this ever gets round London, Bernard Bee will be busy revising things." I know not what he meant by those things he said.

At that point a commotion broke out beyond our rear-facing open windows. We heard threats and blasphemy from an unfamiliar city voice. There followed the unmistakable sound of blows struck. Then more frightened swearing assaulted our ears.

Finally a second voice rumbled, "Pilgrim, ye try my patience. Were it not for my change of Faith, I would by now have torn that offending arm from its joint and flogged you with it. Now stop that kickin', before I lose my control."

Amid the sound of many other windows opening, I said, "Brother Radcliffe? I thought him to be a Quaker.'.."

"A Quaker he became," said Mrs. G. as she led the way down the stairs, "after he went off to war with my brothers. He rose from wagon driver to be Sergeant-Major of the battalion. He saw far too much of war. He managed to escort my elder brother home as the war's end neared even with a shot-up leg. Before shipping back from convalescing the Civil War ended. A poor shell of a man was he then. His friends feared he'd go walk off a cliff. At last, though, he remembered the one of his school teachers he could not intimidate with his youthful hot temper, who controlled him with never a hand lifted. Zachariah Johnston, rest his soul, put Thaddeus Radcliffe on the road to peace. Peace inside and out. He'll not harm whoever fears him. But he'll not let mischief be done, either."

With that we arrived into the shadowy morning, for the sun had not yet cleared the nearby hills. Brother Radcliffe stood at the edge of a brushy area holding a grown man like a rag doll by the fellow's collar. Obviously Brother Radcliffe's face would sport marks for the next few days. Just as obviously, he cared not. Beside me I just heard T.R. stifle an outburst.

Under my breath, I said, "One of the two, is he not?"

"Indeed," came the whispered reply.

"Morning, Mrs. G., friends," Brother Radcliffe greeted us smiling. "Found this misguided pilgrim prowling the bushes. Got lots of matches, and tinder, and candles, and a tin bottle of coal oil. Got to listening to Old Scratch so hard he didn't hear me at all. Nathan, would ye be so kind as to take him in hand, before he kicks my shins again?"

Nathan's handlebar mustache fairly trembled as he put the man's arm into a painful hammerlock and forced him to walk in the direction of the stable.

Mrs. G. stepped forward saying, "Thank you, Thaddeus. Now you've rescued us two days running...."

Before the other could reply there came a yell from the direction of the road. T.R. and I hurried the few steps to get a view across to the stables.

In the middle of the thoroughfare, Nathan hopped up and down on one foot. Keeping his balance caused his grip on the city man to loosen. Suddenly the fellow executed the gymnastic maneuver I believe is called the cartwheel. His arm now untwisted, he struck out at Nathan. Nathan ducked. In doing so he lost his balance, letting go and sprawling to the roadway.

After yesterday I promised myself to be ready for trouble. Without Mary seeing, I'd slipped my service revolver into my jacket pocket. As the troublemaker took his third step towards freedom, I put a bullet into the road in front of him.

"Stop where you are!" I shouted. He stopped. "I'm a decent shot," I continued, "but not good enough to aim for your legs. If I fire again, it will be for your chest."

As I finished speaking, T.R. and I arrived at the fellow's side. I held my pistol steady at his heart. He eyed us with unadulterated hatred.

"Now, my man," began T.R., "I am sure that the great State of New York will have something to say about setting fires in this parkland. And while Brother Radcliffe may not have delivered you a thrashing, his faith will allow court testimony, I believe. Now tell us...."

T.R. told me later that as he spoke his neck began to prickle, and prickle badly. He looked around. Far up the hill beyond Camp Liberty he caught a flash of reflected light as the sun first illuminated the hilltop. All I knew at that point was that he simultaneously yelled, *Watson look out!* as he shoved me to the side.

I heard the crack of a high powered rifle. I allowed the momentum of T.R.'s shove to turn into a sprint for the interior of the stable.

Turning around at the end of my sprint I realized T.R. had dived behind a horse trough. He looked around the end of the thing and down the road to where it curved as it left the area. Another shot missed his head by inches. T.R. rolled back toward the main building of Camp Liberty until he lay against the structure's wall. I had seen what I took for the smoke of the shot far up the hill that the road circled. He now seemed to be out of the direct line of fire.

Before I could turn back toward the hill, a movement above T.R. caught my eye. I re-gripped my revolver, ready to fend off any new threat. A window almost directly above my friend opened. From the opening came a call of "T.R.! T.R.!"

Had Prime Ministers Disraeli or Gladstone appeared at that window I could not have been more surprised than at that moment. For it was

"Watson, look out!"

Mary's voice that reached my ears.

T.R. looked up in near equal astonishment. "Here, Mary!" he said.

I almost died of fright as Mary looked out the window to locate our friend on the ground. Relief washed over me as she withdrew. Then she reappeared calling, "T.R., catch!"

Something long and partly metallic flashed in and out of the morning shadows mixed with the shafts of light, for the sun had just finished cresting that distant hill. I could see that T.R. reached up for the thing. I heard the impact of something hard being caught with both hands. There followed a sound of metal on metal that I could not identify.

A moment later my friend's foot shoved a baggage cart out into the street. Before it stopped moving, the sharpshooter's rifle cracked again. Wood splinters erupted from the cart's deck.

I still looked at the cart when another booming sound assaulted my ears. A quick shift of my eyes informed me of the origin of the earlier strange sound.

For at the corner of the building T.R. leaned against the wall for support as he fired shot after shot with a Winchester lever-action rifle.

Honestly, Holmes, I feel I must pause here. I am going dry from speaking. Let me pour another cup of Mrs. Hudson's fine coffee. Ah, still very warm. We both have seen pictures, and heard descriptions of the Winchester series of rifles, and of their abilities. We saw them demonstrated, after a fashion, in Buffalo Bill's show, but those cartridges were loaded with barely a pinch of powder for safety. I certainly had never seen one fired in anger.

We have also seen our own expert hunters work with their sporting guns. I'd stood by in case of accidents at training where our soldiers practiced the so-called "mad minute." There they fire as many aimed rounds as possible from their bolt action rifles in a fixed period of time. With an experienced squad or platoon that is very impressive.

Ah, that soothes my throat. Holmes, you well know how the mind makes strange connections between and among seemingly unrelated events. As T.R. loosed his second round, for one brief instant I pictured our trip down to Cornwall on that case for the current Earl of Blasie. Remember his grandfather, the Admiral, earned the nickname "Old Blaze-away." That morning in the Adirondacks, T.R.'s rifle rested itself in the deep shadow as he fired up towards a hillside mostly in bright morning sun. In those circumstances fire did indeed blaze away from the muzzle of the Winchester, and at a rate of fire that would leave Her Majesty's best troops gasping in awe.

Five rounds T.R. fired in seemingly not many more seconds. "Bless you, Mary!" he called out as the echoes of the last discharge faded away. "Come, Watson! I doubt I hit him at this range. Put the Fear of God into him. Or so I hope. Duck behind those out buildings. I'll meet you at the road's edge."

A few seconds later he joined me behind an outcropping of rock at the beginning of the hillside. When I looked at the fearsome Winchester, one of Mary's scarves adorned the narrow front of the stock like a knight is said to have worn from his lady.

"So that was in the golf bag. But the scarf?"

"Your Mary does indeed have a cool head on her shoulders," he replied. "She found the boxes of ammunition and tied one to each side of the stock. Put this box in your pocket, in case I lose the other to a tearing branch."

With that he proceeded up the hill beckoning me to follow.

Follow I did. We made our way through saplings, brush, and old forest monoliths. To say I deferred to his woodsmanship is a vast understatement. I know nothing of the character of New World forests, and this was a very thick one.

The early leaves of spring allowed us to see further than later in the year. In full summer I doubt I could have seen ten feet in most areas. Of course, this worked both ways. I scanned all around for signs of our foe.

T.R. must have noticed the swiveling of my head. He whispered, "He headed over the crest of this hill when I fired. We need only be sure he does not circle to our sides."

To the top of the hill we hurried as much as caution would permit. As we approached the crest, T.R. motioned for me to be still while he crawled in near-snake fashion to carefully peer onto the downslope. A moment later he beckoned to me.

A small trail led in the direction of the barely seen road far round from Camp Yankee. With both our eyes scanning the terrain, we hurried as much as we dared. Soon we approached the road, but at some height above it. Just as we discovered a steep path of descent, we heard the clatter of horse's hooves racing away.

T.R. bounded down the steep tail at a near breakneck pace. I followed at the best speed I could make. As the trail ended just off the road, we found ample evidence that a horse had waited there for many hours. Probably all night, if not more. Already we could barely hear the sounds of the racing horse in the distance.

We immediately headed down the road in the direction of Camp Liberty at a trot. Just before the place came into view, T.R. called a halt.

Huffing a bit, he told me, "Do not take chances, my friend, with Yankees who've been shot at."

Taking a deep breath, he stood in the middle of the road to bellow, "Ahoy, Camp Liberty! Watson and Roosevelt coming down the center of the road!"

We walked a few hundred feet. Then a voice a rod or two up the hill called out, "It *is* Watson and Roosevelt. Let pass." Then came a lower voice to us, "Head on in, friends. Should be no trouble for you now."

We called out our own thank yous, then headed down the road at a faster pace. We rounded the bend where the Camp Liberty compound slid into view. No women or children, and few men were visible. All the men we could see carried long hunting guns, or fowling pieces of varying descriptions.

The damaged cart T.R. kicked into the street now carried a cargo. Brother Radcliffe's well found fire starter now lay on the cart. A quick glance told me the first rifle shot had pierced his heart. Two younger men hauled the cart toward one of the smaller out buildings.

The two of us were quickly waved into the Camp office. Here we were greeted by Mrs. G., a slightly limping Nathan, and the redoubtable Brother Radcliffe. After sparse greetings, T.R. related how we traced the rifleman to the road leading more or less west.

"Making for the railhead at Bolton would be my guess," rumbled Brother Radcliffe.

To which T.R. replied, "Is there any chance we can overtake him?"

"Overtake him, or cut him off, no," replied Mrs. G. "But if Thaddeus is willing, there is a chance of reaching Bolton ahead of him. No one knows the byways and shortcuts of these hills and mountains better'n he. You may end up in the middle of a fight, old friend. The choice is fully yours."

Brother Radcliffe's smile held a tenderness I would not have imagined. "Oh, come now, Ester. You know I'll do anything my faith permits for you and your family. I'll see to the mounts, and make sure the good doctor gets Ethan Allen." He winked at me as he strode out the door.

Agreed that our best chance of learning more about this strange turn of events lay in catching the departed horseman, T.R. and I used

the next brief period as we thought best. My friend questioned Mrs. G.
and other family members about the town of Bolton. I hurried over to
the out buildings behind the stable where I did the unnecessary deed of
declaring the fire starter dead. Then I thoroughly rifled his pockets and
clothing. I found the usual coins and humdrum to be expected in most
men's pockets. But I also found two artfully concealed small knives in his
suit coat and tiny derringer-style pistols in each of his boot heels. His thin
wallet yielded some papers whose significance became readily apparent by
day's end.

Mrs. G. agreed to send for the county sheriff in the usual way, but
to say nothing of our expedition to intercept the shooter. By that time
Thaddeus Radcliffe bellowed for us to be off. With more sureness than
the previous day, I mounted Ethan Allen. As T.R. mounted, I took note
that the stable somehow managed to rig a makeshift scabbard for his fast
talking Winchester.

Then off we went. For about a quarter mile we hurried back the way we
entered Warrensburg in the first place. Not far from the point I intercepted
the water wagon, we plunged off the road into what Americans seem to call
a draw that allowed horses in single file to make a fairly easy passage over
and through a modestly sized Adirondack peak. Beyond that, I became as
lost I had been slithering through the City of New York with T.R.

Where my posterior met the saddle soon lost all feeling. We rushed
up. We rushed down. We hurried around. After about an hour, Brother
Thaddeus bid us halt beside the proverbial babbling brook. Here we allowed
the horses a respite and a chance to drink. We also availed ourselves of the
crystal clear and nigh on ice cold water.

"The rougher parts still await us, Pilgrims," observed Brother Radcliffe.
"If I could, I'd change horses here. Restin' the animals is better'n nothing.
T'will save time overall."

"Mrs. G. speaks highly of you," replied T.R. "Obviously, your acquaintance is a long one."

"Nigh on forty years I've known Sweet Ester. Thou would not have
known me then, friends. A regular hellion I was, and her ardent suitor. She
liked me right enough, but wouldn't tolerate the temper that cursed me in
those days. So I lost out to a far better man in Mr. Gordon. A peaceful and
kind man, he was. And could have beat me like a drum had I been too
stupid to understand. Now we'd best get mounted."

As we embarked in the almost invisible trail, I remarked, "Brother
Radcliffe, the few members of the Society of Friends I know in England

no longer use the speech of King James in conversation. If you don't mind my curiosity...."

"My teacher, Zackariah, grew up using it. I started out of respect for him. And to remind myself, and others, I was no longer what I had been. Now, the trail widens. Follow me!"

With that we plunged down a ravine, then ran along a lower ridge line. Not long afterward, we led the nervous horses through the heavy timber doors of a long disused mine. That, our leader noted as we emerged at the other end, saved us more than two miles.

Less than two hours after that we reached the outskirts of Bolton. T.R. and Brother Radcliffe made for the small city police station. Leaving my horse with them, I worked my way through the edge of the forest surrounding the town until I reached the railroad station.

The structure seemed immense, Holmes, given the relatively small size of the permanent population of the Hamlet. "In season," as they call it, whole trainloads of city visitors would arrive to be served and dispersed to any of the dozens of hotels and Great Camps of the region. As you had taught me, such a place has sources of information that most do not comprehend.

I felt unseen eyes on me as I walked up from the woods into the cleared area across from the station. Trying not to look suspicious, I looked along the station's platform. The large facility served only a single main track and an empty siding. About a dozen passengers strolled or stood on the platform. You know the kind who always arrive far too early, my friend. One porter walked slowly up and down, apparently alert for any new request for service. It was obvious that he expected little to do for a time.

As I crossed the main track, I waved cheerfully at the fellow. I'm sure I looked disheveled enough that he did not think me another early arriving passenger. I went round to the far side of the station. As you have observed, Holmes, the arrangement of station facilities of a given size vary but little in the world. I crossed a cleared area with benches and swings for passengers and their children alongside the interior waiting room. Then came the toilets, followed by the offices of the station. Next the area for loading baggage onto carts. And finally a small office and waiting area for the porters and sellers of drinks and papers. Into this I stepped.

An older Negro put down a book and rose from a desk as I entered. "May I help you, sir?"

"Forgive my appearance," I began. "I have just ridden in from Camp Liberty on a most important errand. I wish to speak to all porters and vendors currently here. A crime has been committed at the Camp. My companions are currently informing your authorities. I believe the criminal will try to board the next train to escape the region."

"I can take you to the Station Agent, sir."

"I would prefer not, at this time," I replied. "Chances are he will begin some formal search. The man we seek would notice anything of the sort. He might well decide it better for his health to walk to another region. The people who work out of this office will be far better suited to the task of discovering him, and I ask that they take no action. Simply pass the word."

Pulling out his pocket watch, the fellow said, "The Adirondack Arrow, headed for New York, is due in fifty-seven minutes. But the local train that serves these parts left twelve minutes ago. Might not your quarry be on that?"

"I do not believe so. It is to be hoped that our party arrived just ahead of him," I said with as much conviction as I could.

"May I ask who guided you? Only a local could have made such a thing possible."

"Brother Thaddeus Radcliffe."

"There is no better, sir. Still, I am reluctant...."

At that point I chanced to glance at the shelves of books affixed to the wall next to the fellow's desk. In addition to publications related to the rails, I noticed Hawthorne, Poe, James Fenimore Cooper, and Dickens, among others. All showed much usage. Then, at the end of the lowest shelf, I discovered battered copies of *A Study In Scarlet,* and *The Sign Of The Four.*

I pointed to those volumes, "You enjoy mysteries, I see. I am here about a real mystery. And the crimes involved are arson and murder."

That gave the fellow pause. After a moment of reflection he replied, "Very well. We will proceed, but only until the police arrive. They will have the final say. And woe betide you, sir, if this is a prank. They will not be amused."

"Nor should they be," I replied. "Thank you for your help."

The fellow pulled a cord by the desk. I heard a bell ring in the next room. In a twinkling a lad of about twelve years appeared.

"Lamont," said my companion, "Quietly get everybody, including the toilet attendants, to the back room. Leave only Jeffrey on the platform. Hop to it!" The boy vanished the way he came.

"Well, sir," he continued to me, also gesturing at those books, "I'd wager you wish you could call for assistance upon your countryman, the late

Sherlock Holmes."

I must have stood in shock for several seconds at that. The fellow began to look concerned for me. Finally I threw off the sudden lethargy. From my jacket pocket I pulled the case containing my various credentials.

"Truer words were never spoken, my friend," I told him as I extracted my passport. "For I am Dr. John Watson."

"Now that must have gotten his attention," exclaimed Sherlock Holmes with a smile. He finished filling his pipe, then got it alight. "Romanticized they may be, but your accounts of our activities seem to be even more widespread than I had imagined. On the high seas. A wild western blizzard. And now the back room of a rural American train station. Where next?

"But do return to your narrative. You used my method of gaining information in a train station. I am curious to hear what you told the staff."

"To be sure, Holmes."

***

With the staff assembled I made a point to look them over in a friendly manner. Josiah Brenner, their leader, introduced me, but did not give my name.

"Thank you for coming so quickly," I began. "Yesterday a fire was deliberately set in the staff quarters at Camp Liberty. Just after dawn today a man dressed like a city office worker was caught in the attempt to start another fire. When he made to escape, someone opened fire with a rifle. My companion and I gave chase to the rifleman, but he got away on horseback headed in this direction.

"The first shot from the second man's rifle killed the fire starter. We soon headed here with Brother Radcliffe as our guide. With luck, our quarry has only just now arrived in Bolton. He is a city man who has lived the past day in the woods. He is about as tall as the average man and neither heavy or thin. That is not a very good description, I know.

"What may be more important is his rifle. It is the tool of his evil trade. He will be extremely reluctant to part with it. We saw enough to know that the piece is aimed through a telescope mounted above the barrel. When the man rode through Camp Liberty yesterday, he carried a fancy leather case strapped across his back. The case was at least one hand's width taller than Lamont here.

"In my opinion, the criminal may well discard the leather case. He may also take the rifle apart, so far as is possible. Even so, the barrel alone will be at least this long. Perhaps a bit longer.

"What I wish you to do is simply keep your eyes open for things that are out of place. The man may be alone, but he also may contrive to join a party of travelers. My guess is that he will not want to let whatever contains the rifle out of his own hands.

"Do not take any action if you think you see this man. Just quietly let Mr. Brenner know. I want no one else hurt. Not staff. Not passengers. Are there any questions?"

"Well said, Watson. Well said. I hope you got the desired results."

"Results there were, my friend, and they helped send T.R. and myself deep into the interior of the United States. Many times further than I ever expected."

Josiah Brenner's people departed one or two at a time. The excited chatter of some ended abruptly as they approached the doors to the platform and station interior.

"They appear to be a well disciplined group," I remarked.

"They have to be. Their income depends on it. And Lamont will have a word with Jeffrey. We will soon know of anyone acting strangely. Now wait. Wait, what's this? That is the baggage wagon from the Hotel DeWitt. Last I knew, Gaylord's Smithy was working on it. The DeWitt does not open for a fortnight yet."

We watched surreptitiously as the large wagon jockeyed expertly until only inches separated it from the baggage room door. A hand reached from the building to slide open the wagon's door. We saw no luggage transferred, but instead three sets of feet hurried into the baggage room. Only a moment later T.R. accompanied two locals into the office.

I must admit I had to take a second look to be indeed sure that this was my new friend. He wore a jacket of an out of date European cut. A bowler hat a quarter size too small topped his head. And he carried, of all things, a cello case. I am sure that you can guess what that contained. When I got a good look at his face I bit my tongue and cheek to keep from laughing. Beneath the hat, his hair gleamed of grease and was parted straight atop his head. Someone had waxed his mustache. He looked like a bad caricature of a symphonic musician, and he squinted horribly until he produced and donned his pince-nez.

"Greetings, Watson," he hissed. "I must look even worse than when

Thomas Nast drew me for his rag of a newspaper. Remind me to show that to you some time. "

With T.R., it turned out, were Chief Forbes of the local police and, by good fortune, Mr. Joseph Murray, the County Sheriff. After introductions, my friend reviewed the situation for me.

"With Brother Radcliffe backing my story, and my Federal credentials, I was able to convince these gentlemen not only of the facts of the case, but also the need for secrecy. The killer must believe himself ahead of the word of his crimes. We have the best chance of catching him here."

And so it began. The search remained hidden from the Station Master, or Agent. The man was known to be honest and efficient, but also was he known to bustle about decrying any little change from routine. Over the next half hour about two dozen additional passengers arrived. Some already possessed their tickets. Others bought them, as well as magazines and foodstuffs. Murray, the County Sheriff, commented that at the season's height over two hundred souls could be found on the platform.

Fifteen minutes from train time Jeffrey stepped into the office. He looked briefly startled as he recognized the officials with us.

He nodded to them, but addressed me. "You be the one asking for help, sir?" At my nod he continued. "There's a smooth fellow parked right in the middle of the passengers. His pants been brushed and his shoes cleaned up, not polished. But both been hard worn lately. They fit right. His suit coat don't quite match the pants. Not a real good fit, either, and its spring cleaning fresh. Got about the biggest carpetbag they make. Not much in it, but its stretched whatcha call catercorner. Stretched so far the strap's like to tear from the buckle tongue. Keeps the bag between his feet. Not to one side, like most folks. That help, sir?"

"Sounds very promising, Jeffrey," I replied. "Does he appear nervous?"

"Not to most people, no indeed. Cool as melting snow water. Underneath he's a holding himself tight. I could feel it. Sent young Felix by him sellin' peanuts and candy. He felt like I did. High strung, no end."

T.R. and I consulted with the local officials. We peered through two cracked doors onto the platform. Then the County Sheriff commented that with the rifle stowed, our suspected man might not be armed.

I dug into my left hand coat pocket. From it I produced the knives and tiny pistols. "The man who died at Camp Liberty carried these," I told him. "I do not doubt the man who killed him is similarly prepared for trouble. We need some way to get the true passengers away from him."

Not three minutes later Jeffrey emerged from the Station Office's door back onto the platform. He carried a small wooden crate. He walked to where he could be heard by any passengers in the wooded area to the rear.

There he called out, "Ladiesss and Gentlemennnn! One of the local folks found some valuables on the road to the Langley Hotel. The same road most of you came here on. The train being due they hurried along to th' station. Please be so kind as to step over here and see if you can help identify what we have."

Most of the passengers headed towards Jeffrey, for a diversion, I suppose, if nothing else. Our target watched them go. At that point, Chief Forbes stepped from the baggage room door casually moving to the far side of our target. Even with T.R.'s disguise, neither of us dared show our faces at that point. The cello case stood empty as my friend crouched by the cracked door with his Winchester at the ready.

Forbes, a native to these parts, did not carry the air of a policeman about him. He managed to place himself between our target and the closest line into the thick woods before the man became concerned. He glanced around. Only a tiny tightening of his lips indicated additional tension. Then he noted a uniformed officer crossing the road to the center of town about one hundred yards away.

The man's head swiveled left and right. As Chief Forbes drew breath to speak, his face hardened. Our suspect's hand flew under his coat and behind his back. The coat's tail flapped up revealing to us in the staff office the butt of the pistol he tugged free of his belt.

I yanked the door fully open. T.R. took one step out as he brought his Winchester to firing position.

Immediately following the rifle's roar came a yelp of pain. I peered around the door to see T.R.'s target spinning around from the bullet now lodged deep in his shoulder.

Over the next few minutes, the Passengers at the Bolton station had the dubious privilege of enduring the most comprehensive session of off-the-cuff swearing I could remember. In or out of the military, by the bye. The man swore as he was searched. Swore as I prevented him from bleeding to death. Swore as handcuffs affixed him to a heavy wooden chair. Swore as the chair was moved into the baggage room of the station. Then Chief Forbes asked his name. He never spoke again in my hearing. Much later, I'm told, he began demanding the presence of a certain New York City attorney-at-law of high skills and low morals.

The man gave us no information. What he wore and carried did. The not quite matching suit coat yielded local laundry marks. Forbes used the station's telephone to dispatch an officer to the home of the garment's owner. At my suggestion, another officer scoured all the trash burning pits and barrels in that home's immediate area.

We did not reach Camp Liberty again until well into the evening.

**

"When I received Ashley's letter about meeting you, Mr. Roosevelt," said Mrs. G., "I realized I'd been guilty of the same thing as my father. I kept the story of the family's journey here too much a secret. Had I not done so, Ashley would have told you nothing at all.

"Ashley's letter told me that trouble might follow. Not from you directly, but the world now knows of Mary's existence. And her father's lineage is of public record in England. Then came that damnable speculation in the Comet. With that I mailed my father's envelope, hidden in a package of clothing made by his mother, to Ashley. I told him much of what I have told you. I asked him to hide it safely away for six months. If he hadn't heard more from me by then he was to bring it back here at that time. Now that trouble has indeed come I shall telegraph him...."

"Do not do that, Mrs. G.," I interrupted. "I do not believe we can trust the telegraph in this matter."

That brought the conversation to an abrupt halt. Holmes, I'd often wondered what it felt like to suddenly become the center of attention when you would drop a verbal bombshell on a case. Now I found out. Mrs. G., her family members, and Brother Radcliffe, sat silent. I could see some of them fumbling for words.

A moment later T.R. sputtered, "Not trust the telegraph? Watson, please explain."

I do not have your certainty of facts and conclusions when you reach them, my friend. I did not care much for being the absolute focus of everyone's attention. To give myself a bit of additional thinking time I pulled a folder out of the small valise I'd obtained in Bolton. I made a great show of opening the folder inside and spreading out part of the contents on the table we sat around. All the while my mind rushed along like an Alpine avalanche.

"These are the written and printed documents we found on the persons of the two criminals. T.R., better than I, can verify that they traveled by rented horse to Warrensburg the day of the fire, and for some part of the journey as companions, not chance-met travelers. From Chief Forbes we learned that the fire starter first visited the Records Office at what you call the County Seat. Here he apparently looked up birth and property records related to the name Morstan. That finished, he hurried to Warrensburg. Because our coach made an unscheduled stop, he was able to catch up with the shootist and they traveled together for a time.

"Before leaving the County Seat, the fire starter telegraphed a one line message to a New York City telegraph office. The message mentions missing his girlfriend. Probably one or two of the words constitute a report of what he discovered in the public records. He waited for a reply that came within five minutes. That means his 'girlfriend' waited for his message and replied post-haste. He received an endearment in reply and practically dashed to rent a horse and ride out.

"Both men had near identical copies of our railway itinerary, and the form of the copies is astonishing. A member of T.R.'s household requested the bookings, as I think you call it, while out and about on his regular errands for the Roosevelts. When the agent at that rail station finished setting up the itinerary, he sent a telegram directly to T.R. The tickets themselves followed by messenger. T.R. showed me the telegram. I took special note because the format was somewhat different than that used in the British Isles.

"The captured itineraries are virtually identical to the form of that telegram. Somewhere, somehow, whoever is behind this managed access to that message. And the station of the booking is far from the only spot where the tickets could be requested. Either a group watched and followed every person, family and staff to leave the Roosevelt home that day without notice, or they have access to telegrams that no honest man should.

"Sherlock Holmes often told me to eliminate the impossible. Then what remains, however unlikely, must be true. Following all comers and goers from the busy Roosevelt family and their retainers without any notice seems impossible to me. Therefore I must conclude that the person behind this damnable affair has near total access to telegraph messages."

Of course, my theory further escalated the feeling of the fox in the henhouse for the good people of Camp Liberty. After the bones of the known facts of the case were picked clean, the discussion turned to matters of security and the proper running of the Camp. As such things needed immediate implementation by the Camp's staff, the three of us soon withdrew for the night.

Back in our suite, T.R. and I soon reached one inescapable conclusion.

"So we agree, Watson," T.R. summed up. "The contents of that sealed envelope must be discovered at the earliest possible instant. Mr. Ashley Morstan needs to be warned in any case. He may soon come into danger even if no one suspects he has the letter. Lacking use of the telegraph, someone must proceed post-haste to the Dakotas to retrieve the thing. Our Postal service to that area is slow. A party needs to set forth immediately.

"I must go. I am responsible for stirring this pot of trouble in the first place, and I know something of the territory. Forgive me, Mary, but I believe your husband should accompany me. The Morstans will trust him as a member of the family, and he is well versed in rough travel. In addition, he is the only one available to us with any training at all as a detective. That may well be needed, not to mention his understanding of things English that might be invaluable when that confounded envelope is opened."

I immediately felt the need to agree with T.R., but I tried to give no indication. Instead I looked to Mary. I could see that she was disturbed, but hardly shocked by what our friend said.

After a moment I said, "I fear T.R. has the right of it, my dearest. Any threat to your whole family must be met. First we must find a safe place for you...."

I got no further than that. With a boldness I knew lurked beneath her usually placid manner, Mary spoke out. I took no small private pleasure in watching Theodore Roosevelt's jaw slowly drop open at her words.

"Nonsense, John. Would you 'get me to a nunnery' when the rest of my family faces peril? No indeed! Finally I have again some family of my own, and worthy people by all we've seen. If they will have me, I will stay here. With them. And I shall earn my place in one manner or another. Unless there is some experienced adventurous family member not yet known to us, you and T.R. are the proper ones to make the journey. Much as it distresses me, I understand that. You knew I worried when you continued to accompany Sherlock Holmes after we wed. But I did not try to dissuade you. I, of all people, knew what good came from such forays. Now, here again, the game is afoot. And you would rise to help these people even were I not related to them. That is a part of your nature that Mr. Holmes brought into the light. Now, my wonderful husband and gallant knight, you must ride an iron charger into this nation's wild west. And I shall await your return."

And that, old friend, was certainly that.

The following morning plans were laid, information was exchanged and packing done. This included both T.R. and myself in writing a summary of what was known, plus our suspicions, regarding the outrageous manner. These writings a family member took to a Post Office more than twenty miles distant. There he posted the envelope to a little known friend of T.R.'s. Said friend would re-post the contents to an address given to us by Detective Walter Brooks.

At about the same time, I mounted Ethan Allen yet again. As we said our profound good-byes, Mary informed me that an experienced British governess was considered a major asset by many of the Camp's social climbing clientele. And a governess for younger children Mary would be again, under the name of Sanders. We then headed off once more under the guidance of Brother Thaddeus Radcliffe.

On this trip stealth, not speed, best served out purposes. Our guide took us through paths untrod in recent times. We crossed roads only with extreme caution not to be seen. Some hours later we passed the boundary of the Adirondack Park. The hand of man became much more apparent soon thereafter. We skirted farmland and circled hills stripped bare of timber, though some such had been replanted.

Not long before sunset we reached a sawmill of some size situated on the end of a rail spur. A train of about twenty cars lurched forward as we dismounted so that another flat-bedded car could be loaded with bundles of rough-cut lumber and tall, barely trimmed logs. T.R. and I remained in a draw while Brother Thaddeus visited the place. He soon returned.

"Friends," he began, "the father of the train's engineer marched off to war with me and the Morstan brothers. Now 'Uncle' Thaddeus' friends may ride with him and none but his loyal fireman be the wiser. The engine'll be out of sight of the mill by the time the final car begins to load. That's your boarding call. Ye may be a bit cramped in the engine cab. Next stop: the main line at Glens Falls."

And so it was. We gave Brother Radcliffe our sincere thanks as he took charge of our horses. Soon the train headed off into the late afternoon. The journey of about four hours seemed even shorter as the engineer "nephew" made us welcome like old friends. I paid particular attention to the engine controls as they were unlike those on English rail engines that I had seen. These he explained as best he could over the general roaring of the pistons and firebox alike.

That part of our trip far and away turned out to be the most interesting and pleasant of the lot. Not that most others were unpleasant, but mostly because of the vastness of the United States of America. Later on I discovered that the "as the crow flies" distance from our starting point to Deadwood in South Dakota far exceeded twelve hundred miles, and would that we could have joined said crow in the air. For by rail the distance was far longer, so long that I have never had the ambition to calculate the measure with accuracy.

At the station on the main line, T.R. used his cold cash and Federal credentials to secure us passage in the baggage car of a westbound passenger train. A mistake as it turned out. For the conductor, an honest man, telegraphed the event to his supervisor, but we only discovered this much later.

The following morning we quietly departed that train at a medium sized town in Pennsylvania. We hired a small cart to take us the few miles to yet another railroad company's tracks and station. There we bought tickets to the city of Chicago. In the hours before the arrival of our new train we ate a fine meal at a restaurant serving, in part, the food of the Czech people. Then we made use of the local bath house, and each bought a change of clothing that T.R. told me better befitted the areas through which we would next pass. We did not try to sleep. T.R. unnecessarily told me to save that for the train. We wandered the town aimlessly. I found the time well spent learning more about how yet another part of the sprawling United States of America lives.

An hour before our departure we ate another meal at a tavern. We were treated well by all we met. As we walked the few blocks back to the station, I mentioned that my English accent caused little comment.

"That is no real surprise to me, Watson," replied T.R. "People from many parts of the world pass through here by train. Unless some English Johnnie made serious trouble in town recently, few will take more than a passing interest. Ah, just two more streets, I reckon. See, the tracks are visible between those houses."

We walked on without speaking further. As the last cross street approached, we began to see the opened graveled area where carts, buggies, even a few bicycles and a single motorcar parked. Then one end of the station hove into view.

That one end was all I observed when T.R. halted mid-stride. Suddenly I found myself pressed against the brick wall of the building we passed.

"Relax, Watson," hissed T.R. "Pretend that I tripped. We have a problem.

A potential problem, anyway."

"Do you have your balance now?" I said aloud. Putting my head down I whispered, "What did you see?"

"Two men who look to be Pinkerton Agents stand by the station doors. You've heard of the Pinkerton's, no doubt. But I doubt your English press recounts some of the darker exploits of the breed. These days companies hire them for ruthless strike-breaking and other barely legal deeds. A far cry from their early reputation. I've even seen government reports suggesting a secret cadre who carry false credentials so that they may be disowned at need if their transgressions become too outrageous. These men may be on some errand unrelated to us, but we dare not take such a chance."

"Shall we take another train? Or another route?" I asked.

"If they do search for us, we have left little doubt we have been in this town. We need to vanish, like a magician's puff of smoke. Let us walk back the way we came as we consider our options."

We walked to a part of the town's business district we had not previously explored. I looked around at the signs of various establishments for ideas and inspiration. I chuckled a bit at the candy kitchen with an arrow pointing to the office of a dentist above it. A dry goods emporium and a haberdasher's offered no obvious help. Then, across the street, and a block down, I saw it.

The wide two story building sported a permanent sign depicting three linked rings and the letters "I.O.O.F." But that was not what caught my eye. Tied to that sign and draping down a full yard, a heavy canvas banner proclaimed "EZEKIEL'S REPERTORY PLAYERS: This Week Only." A large enclosed wagon similarly marked stood in front of building.

"There," I said, "may be our puff of smoke."

A few moments later, Holmes, we stood in the Lodge building of the American version of our own Odd Fellows order. Therein we met Ezekiel Hodgens, owner and director of a traveling company of players. Once convinced we represented neither his creditors, nor an outraged father or husband, he became most happy to assist us—for a fee, of course.

After a brief discussion, he produced basic hand-stitched black pants, white shirts of similar making, braces, and equally basic shoes. One of his players dug out two coats to roughly fit us. They were quickly shorn of any decorative buttons. Hats similar to that worn by brother Radcliffe came next. Soon other members of the troop began minor alterations on

"Two men who look to be Pinkerton Agents stand by the station doors."

the clothing. Then Ezekiel commenced the application of spirit gum to our faces.

Soon T.R. and I sported full beards running from ears to chin leaving the cheeks bare. They were good quality false whiskers, I might add. Only a close inspection would reveal them. With less than twenty minutes having passed we paid the grinning Ezekiel and bade his troop farewell. Our small bags in our hands once more, we walked to the station.

Out of earshot of all I whispered, "T.R., just who are we supposed to be?"

"Men of the Amish religious sect," he replied. "They originated in the Germanic states or Switzerland. Perhaps both. They are hard working farmers who speak some kind of German dialect among themselves, as I understand. They do not mingle with outsiders more than absolutely necessary. I think I can produce something resembling their accenting of English. You might do well to remain mute in this situation. Once free of scrutiny I imagine we can become ourselves again. The sooner, the better, for my conscience. For the Amish, above all else, are pacifists. I have no wish to cast a stain on their faith's reputation."

We calmly walked past the two men that T.R. had observed at the walkway into the station grounds. You would have observed far more than I did, my friend, but I knew in the first instant that these were hunters, and very dangerous ones.

About two dozen people stood with us by the tracks. We kept apart from the others while pretending to chat. As we heard the approaching train in the distance, the hunters joined us.

When the train stopped, we joined the queue to board. We found end seats facing forward in an uncrowded car. The hunters boarded the first passenger car and walked through. T.R. and I continued to whisper nonsensical chatter to each other as they passed. As the train began its lurching start, I glanced back to see the two men back on the platform. To this day I have no idea who they really sought.

About ninety minutes later our train stopped at an even smaller town. The style of buildings differed markedly from where we embarked. I eagerly took in the sights. A little too eagerly, as it turned out.

Soon after we again rolled down the rails. We heard the door open as someone entered our car from the one behind us. Seconds later a large man of about fifty years squatted beside our seats. He was dressed much as we were, but his garments looked far heavier than our stage costumes.

"I do not know who you are," he said quietly in a slight Germanic accent, "but you are not Amish, or even Mennonite. I could see that from the station platform. Please make me sure that you mean no one harm and I say nothing of this."

Theodore Roosevelt can be blunt, brash, and extremely dangerous, but here I saw his abilities as a diplomat. "We must apologize, sir," he whispered. "I know that your people want little to do with any government, but here are my papers as a member of the United States Federal Government. And I would swear or affirm to you, in your chosen form, that we travel to prevent harm to a number of people. We then realized that someone might be watching for us on this train. What you see was the only disguise available to us. And again, I apologize to you and all members of your faith. We will remove our disguises as soon as it seems safe to do so."

"Very well, English. I will say nothing. You fool no one who knows my people. Not at all."

"Thank you, sir," said T.R. "May I ask what we have done that is not correct?"

"Of course, English," he whispered with a smile. "A young Amish man shaves his face. When he marries he grows the beard like mine. The Amish have no 'styles' as I think you say. The married man grows the beard, but never any mustache like the two of you. That is not plain."

At that point I felt I had to ask, "Pardon me, sir. Why do you call my friend 'English?'"

As the man rose to leave, he said, "That is what we call all who are not Amish."

***

Chicago. I wish I could have seen more of it. On the train both into and out of the city, no trace remained of the huge conflagration of a generation earlier. T.R. startled me by revealing that the city's monicker as "The Windy City" came not from her weather, but sprang from the loquaciousness of her political speakers. Here we divested ourselves of almost all things Amish. In fact, we encountered the American Division of General Booth's Salvation Army near the train station. To their work we gladly donated the clothing we no longer needed. We ate at an establishment called the Harvey House before boarding our next train, and then we were headed westward again.

At the station in a small farming town of the state known as Iowa, I walked the platform for most of the five minutes of the stop. I chanced upon a fellow waiting for a train in the opposite direction. I traded him Deadwood Dick's inaugural adventure for two much read copies of Buffalo Bill's supposed histories. As he put the Nickel Library away, I noticed a corner of a copy of The Strand in his bag. I remarked on it. He told me he did not intend to part with it for it contained "The Final Problem." Before I could comment further, my train's conductor bellowed, *"All Aboard!"*

I hurried back to my seat. Surprised I was not to find T.R. there ahead of me. I looked back to the platform. Just as the porter removed the step up to the train's stairs, T.R. raced from the interior of the station carrying a canvas bag full of I knew not what. He sprang aboard just before the car took its first lurching movement forward. A moment later he eased himself into the seat beside me.

He huffed a bit before saying, "I bought a few things at the station's store, Watson, and I've mailed off a few more lines to my friend. Just in case."

Again, Holmes, I must remark on the size of the United States. By the time I made that exchange of story papers, we had traveled about the straight line distance from London to Budapest, and still had hundreds of miles to go—and for the most part in the southern region of the state of South Dakota.

After that stop, the farm fields and forests gave way to plains and rolling hills, and eventually some of what we in England would call mountains came into view. T.R. firmly assured me that these, compared to the Sierra and Rocky Mountain chains, were but the "foothills" known as the Black Hills. Thus we entered the area said to be the habitat of Deadwood Dick. Our tickets, however, could carry us to a town far past the area of Deadwood. No sense in declaring our intentions, as T.R. said.

On our last train, T.R. struck up a conversation with our train's conductor. The fellow obviously knew his business. He did much to keep his passengers happy and amused, all the while firmly enforcing the rules and standards of the Line. At odds with our previous efforts not to be noticed, I questioned T.R. about it.

"I am applying liberal amounts of butter to his bread, Watson," he told me. "I have a big favor to ask of him before we leave this train. There is a place somewhat past Deadwood where trains will pick up known passengers from the local ranches who wait by the tracks. What is sometimes called a 'whistle stop.' I shall propose that we get off there."

"Such an arrangement does not seem particularly safe out here," I replied. "Or have I been reading too many of your Nickel Libraries?"

"Not at all, my friend. The gangs that operate out of the Hole-In-The-Wall are quite real, and bold. But you will see that the place has a safety granted by God's own hand, and every member of the train crew will have his hand on a weapon during the stop."

The train paused at Deadwood, South Dakota, just before dawn. At T.R.'s insistence we pretended to doze through the meal stop.

Just over an hour later the train came to a halt as it crested a long low hill. T.R. and I alighted with our small bags. We stood on a dirt road which crossed the tracks at near a right angle. The engineer blew a couple of long blasts on the engine's steam whistle before the train rolled away from us.

Then I looked around. Once more, T.R. had the right of it. For seemingly God himself took a hand in the building of this unusual hill. The ground gently sloped away from us in all directions. Anyone aboard a train could see for at least half a mile any way they cared to look across a land without dips, ravines, or any other hiding place. No trees, and only light brush, grew on the gentle slopes.

On the other side of the tracks lay two rough hewn wooden benches. We walked (I believe they say "sauntered" in those parts) across the tracks and sat down. T.R. immediately opened his traveling case.

"Welcome to Wilson's Bench, Watson. I'm sure the senior officers of our recent railroad believe that this is a new small town. Hence, a whistle stop where the train whistles to warn passengers to hurry, for the train will not stop unless passengers are seen waiting. In actuality the place sits amid a number of large ranches. If passengers are here, they raise a signal pole down the track for the train to stop. In our case, the engineer kindly gave a loud whistle to rouse the Wilson ranch, it being the nearest. Therefore this place's name. We shall tarry a bit, but should no one come, we will have to do an amount of walking."

As he spoke, T.R. pulled a number of wax sealed items and packages from his case. I assisted in breaking them open. Before not too much longer than it takes to tell, he fully assembled his Winchester Model 1876.

"Now I feel a bit safer," he said as he worked a few rounds through the weapon's action. Satisfied, he leaned the piece against the bench to dig into the canvas sack. He handed me a large canteen full to the brim with water. "Be glad it is still spring, Watson. Summers here can be trying to one used to your damp English climate."

"I doubt even this place can rival the summer of Afghanistan, my friend. Most of our weather thermometers cracked or simply shattered in the shade, much less the direct sun. Still, I take your point. I say, is that a dust devil, or is somebody approaching around that far bend in the road?"

Rounding the bend came that small cloud of dust, and soon we could make out a wagon drawn by a pair of horses. One more saddle horse followed, reins tied to the vehicle's end. Surely you have seen drawings of the rig in magazine illustrations and photographs, Holmes, what the Americans call a buckboard.

Two men in Stetson hats with colorful shirts rode on the wagon's seat. At about one hundred yards distance one of them pulled out a pair of binoculars. T.R. apparently expected such an action, for he quietly urged me to join him in moving away from the benches and the Winchester. With our move, the wagon sped up a bit to finally stop between ourselves and the benches.

One of the men riding the buckboard seemed as thin as a skeleton with skin. The other almost seemed fat, but I could see cords of muscles surface when he moved his limbs.

"Tarnation," said the thin one, "Ah came out here expectin' ta find somebody important. Not two dudes what got thrown offa the train."

I was not sure what to make of things, but T.R. just laughed. "And a good morning to you, too, Oliver. I see you are still Jack Sprat himself."

"Roosevelt! Land o' Goshen, I thought somethin' looked familiar about you. Never see'd you in city clothes before. 'S okay, Stanley. Thanks fer ridin' shotgun."

Without a word the heavyset man sprang from the buckboard, mounted the following horse, and departed cross country. We climbed aboard in his place. I became acquainted with this Oliver on our way to the Wilson Ranch and a fine breakfast.

***

Less than two hours later we followed the same road down the other side of the strange hill on borrowed horses. You would have hardly recognized me, Holmes. We both wore well used—but clean—garments of the cowboy, including boots and Stetson hats. Uriah Wilson, it seemed, started his working life at sea. After hearing our story, he furnished us clothing from his "slops chest," the Navy's term for issued garments. In this case, a hodge-podge of things left behind by departed ranch employees.

Oliver left the ranch at the same time on his twice-a-week run to

Deadwood for supplies. This time he also carried a shopping list for our party mixed in with the ranch's needs.

T.R. seemed born to the western saddle, and I was getting a bit used to it. I felt just a trifle nostalgic as my service revolver rested in a flapped holster once part of some American Cavalry soldier's uniform. The pinned flap was necessary as my revolver was not a good fit.

T.R. kept touching the low-slung holster he wore, for it was not the style he favored. The Colt .45 double-action revolver he was indeed familiar with. So we rode through the beautiful brisk spring morning. T.R. traveled with great ease, while I threatened to do my neck harm as I tried to observe anything and everything new to me.

After about three hours we paused at a cairn of rocks at a splitting of the trail. (Few Englishmen could call the thing a road, except by charity.) Outside the main pile of stones, a large rock served as a pointer for each branch. Incised into each were puzzling hieroglyphs. I recognized the one pointing behind us, for the intertwined Ws were also on the sign proclaiming welcome at the Wilson ranch. T.R. translated the others for me.

"The left fork is the one we want, Watson. These are the ranches' brands. The horizontal line is read as the word 'Bar.' Wilson's is known as the 'Double W.' The 'S' above 'F' with the line between is the 'S Bar F' ranch, our destination. Someone has had a little fun at newcomers' expense on the third rock. The fallen tree stands for the town of Deadwood. But first you must pass through the 'Bar 20' ranch."

After resting our horses briefly, we pressed on. Not long after that another road joined the main one. A small sign announced the S-Bar-F Ranch. T.R. commented that the sign probably saved his small party's life as they sought shelter from that raging blizzard. Soon we rode into the busy compound of a working ranch. Those going about their various tasks quickly recognized T.R. and called out greetings.

Those shouts soon brought Homer Bennett, the owner, out of the house. "Welcome back, Mr. Roosevelt," he said as he cordially shook T.R.'s hand, "and thank you very much for the set of china you sent. The wife loves it. You didn't really have to do that."

"Nonsense, Mr. Bennett. Your hospitality saved lives. With little chance I could repay that by hosting you in New York, it seemed the least I could do. Unfortunately, we arrive at your gate on urgent business. My companion is married to a third cousin of Ashley Morstan. We must speak with him as soon as possible."

"Today is Ashley's off day," replied Bennett. "He'll be at the north-line's shack a'drawing or painting. Calls that old place his studio. Darn fine painter he is, too. Good chance he's got some young 'lady' up there to pose for him." A leering wink accompanied that last part, Holmes.

Directions obtained, we rode the three miles to the "line shack," that being a cabin to shelter ranch hands working away from their usual accommodations. T.R. told me that such things are common, so big are American cattle ranches.

The shack sat on the side of a hill away from the prevailing winds. As we followed the faint trail to it I tried to observe the varied forms of nature thereabout. A bit of movement caught my attention.

"Look there, T.R., down in that small valley. Two horses with but one rider."

"A runaway, by the look of it, and someone in pursuit. Ah, there is that tooth shaped rock Bennett spoke of. We should see the shack in a moment."

And so it was. We crested a small rise. Below us a bit stood a cabin fashioned of old lumber about twenty feet square. Smoke drifted from a large stove pipe in the roof. That same lumber formed a corral behind the place. Two horses occupied the affair which could easily hold twenty. A saddle rested atop the fence and a tiny buggy sat near the gate.

As we headed our horses down towards the cabin front, a horrible sight came into view. An unmoving man lay on the ground not far from the cabin door. Even at some distance I could see what appeared to be a considerable amount of blood on the ground.

"Is that..." I began as we drew back on our reins.

"No, Watson. That man is far too heavy to be Ashley Morstan. Be ready to bolt, my friend," replied T.R. Then he drew a full breath to bellow, *"Halllooo, the shack!"*

We could just barely see the front of the place. A moment later the door opened a crack. The barrel of some sort of weapon eased out and a woman's strong voice called out, "Who be you?"

"Friends of Ashley Morstan!" roared T.R.

"How do I know that?"

"You don't, but Mr. Bennett sent us here. He said there might be a lady posing for him. We mean no one any harm."

"I'll take a chance," came the reply. The voice seemed both determined and worried. "Com'on slowly. With your gun belts on your saddle horns. Move funny and you get the same as that dry gulching buzzard!"

Down we rode with our right hands raised and the other holding the reins. We passed the body. The man had received a load of large sized shot in the face and neck. We tied our horses to a wood hitching rail by the door.

"Two horses stood together where the man lies," said T.R. "Then they bolted."

"Damn right they bolted," came the woman's voice. "Sorry to say they probably took a pellet or two apiece. Now who be you?"

With that she stepped from the cabin. Rock steady in her hands a double barreled shotgun pointed straight at us. She wore nothing but a tattered sheet wrapped around her like a Roman toga. Her red hair had been coiffured above her long neck, but now it was coming loose. Her comely face and hands were blood stained, but that face held a hardness and determination rarely seen on a woman.

"I am Theodore Roosevelt. I met Ashley Morstan a few months ago. We came to talk to him...."

From inside the shack came a weak male voice, "Angel... Angela, I know him...." The sound trailed off as if exhausted.

"Ashley!" she exclaimed. She lowered the shotgun and hurried into the cabin.

On the floor by the door lay Ashley Morstan. Blood stained a makeshift bandage on his chest. He looked deathly pale. Kneeling, I felt for his pulse. It was stronger than I expected it to be. "Get me some blankets," I exclaimed. "He is about to go into shock."

"My friend is a doctor," said T.R. as he yanked the covers from a nearby cot. These he passed to me. "What happened here?"

"I was a posing for him. Only he calls it 'modeling.' When we heard a 'hallo, the shack' from outside, I pulled this sheet around me and peeked out the window. I saw some dude an' Hatchet Face Hogan ridin' up. Didn't like the looks of either one of them. When Ashley stepped out, I grabbed the shotgun. No pockets, so like my daddy used to, I held two more shells in my teeth. The varmints rode up. Asked if he was Ashley Morstan. Soon's he nodded, Hogan drew and shot him.

"I jumped out an' let fly at Hogan. Then at the dude. An' both horses took off. Know I hit the dude, but he's further away than Hogan. Time I reloaded, Hogan's on the ground a'bleeding an' not moving. I grabbed his gun and tended to Ashley."

Soon T.R. galloped off to bring assistance. Young Morstan drifted in and out of consciousness. The wound in his mid-chest had not bled much. I feared he might be losing blood on the inside. I examined the bullet hole. The blood had coagulated to a degree I normally associated with the passage of a day, not the hour, or less, that had transpired. Then I noticed a small metal medical case behind the door.

"Miss Angela," I inquired, "did you find this in the cabin?"

"It's mine, Doctor. Nobody in these parts travels outside of town without packing for trouble. Not them that wants to stay alive anyway. Always got a blanket, pemican, a canteen, and that box under my buggy seat."

Guessing that pemican must be some kind of food, I asked, "How did you stop the bleeding so thoroughly?"

She picked up a small screw top metal can and brought it to me. "This is something an old Indian medicine man showed my daddy how to make. Stops bleeding like magic. I packed th' bullet hole with it. Never heard tell of anybody's hurt gettin' septic after using it, neither."

Cautiously I smelled of the can. My eyes instantly watered. Good gracious, Holmes. I never learned the formula, but any self-respecting germ must run for its life from the concoction.

About that time, Ashley Morstan awoke more fully than before. He looked at Angela, then at me with some fear in his eyes. "Who... Who're you?" he whispered.

"I am Dr. John Watson, married to your third cousin, Mary," I replied. "Theodore Roosevelt and I arrived a bit too late to protect you. But Miss Angela here has put an end to the man who shot you, and did much to keep you alive.

"You must not strain yourself," I continued as I pulled out my credentials case. "Your aunt, Mrs. Gordon, or Mrs. G., sent us to warn you and retrieve the sealed letter she sent you. Here is the letter she gave us before we left Camp Liberty."

With a weak but steady hand he took the letter. I stood and walked away to give him a moment's privacy. Only then did I take time to look around the cabin. On every bit of wall space hung pencil sketches, pen and ink drawings, and not a few oil paintings. On an easel sat a large canvas. A fine nude study of Miss Angela had been mostly laid in with a hard pencil. This young man showed much talent and an apparent love for this unusual part of God's own Earth.

A moment or two later Angela called me back to Ashley's side. As I knelt again at his side, Ashley spoke, "I made an envelope outta some canvas. Sealed the letter in it with wax. Mr. Bennett's holding it for me."

"Thank you, Ashley," I replied. "You rest now. T.R. and I will answer any questions you have after that bullet is out of you."

There the three of us waited. I related how T.R.'s letter brought Mary and myself to the Americas. How much Ashley actually heard or remembered, I knew not, but the narrative helped all of us pass the time. The clatter of approaching horses brought that to a stop.

Angela, now fully dressed, snatched up the shotgun as I drew my service revolver. Nearly as quickly we put the weapons away, for T.R. led Mr. Bennett and two others down the slope to the shack. With them they brought a stretcher. Soon Ashley rested on it, well wrapped from the chill. As the wait for a slower buckboard began, Mr. Bennett sent his two well-armed cowhands on the trail of the "dude" and the two horses.

I folded a spare blanket under my posterior to ride in the back of the buckboard with Ashley. Angela followed in her rig. For much of the journey, T.R. rode beside the buggy politely pressing Miss Angela for additional information. Fortunately, the expert driver kept Ashley from bouncing around excessively. I'll not bother you, Holmes, with the details of the ride into the town of Deadwood, save to say that Mr. Bennett's hands joined us with Hatchet Faced Hogan's horse. No sign of the dude, they told us.

Deadwood, South Dakota, is situated in small valleys set between a series of rolling hills. Not far from the center of the young city, we reached the office and surgery of Dr. Kenneth Marley. I explained the situation to my new colleague. In the end, I administered the ether to Ashley as Marley—far from a stranger to bullet wounds—worked to remove the offending piece of lead.

The rest of our party split up. Mr. Bennett went to see the town sheriff. T.R. and the buckboard's driver began polling the many livery stables seeking where "a dude" had rented a horse that day. One of the two cowboys remained as a guard. The other began making the rounds of the few other doctors' offices looking for a man with buckshot wounds.

Even with the surgery windows open, the fumes from the ether rendered me a bit dizzy. I sat on the back steps of the place until my head cleared. Fortunately, I felt very nearly normal again when that whirlwind named Theodore Roosevelt burst from the door behind me.

"Ah, Watson, there you are. Come on, man! Mr. Bennett's driver thinks he has located that infernal dude."

And so we went. Back aboard our horses we headed for an establishment known as The Fairfield Hotel. Among the most expensive hostelry in the young city, the Fairfield claimed to offer the amenities of a big city hotel.

"And more snobbishness than most locals can tolerate, as I recall," observed T.R. "We'll get little help from the front desk. Except maybe at gunpoint. We shall therefore try Mr. Holmes' method of gaining information."

Our horses hitched several doors away, T.R. and I proceeded in the barren alley between the rows of buildings. Long before we arrived at the delivery and staff entrance of the hotel, several varieties of tobacco smoke reached our noses. Four employees of the establishment sat upon old kegs smoking pipes and cigars.

"Gentlemen," began T.R. as he juggled several gold coins in his half-closed hand, "my friend and I need information...."

Five minutes later one of the four let us into an empty second floor guest suite. Silently we crossed the room to let ourselves out on the balcony that circled only these, the most expensive rooms in the place. Crouching low, we silently moved past a certain number of windows. We then rose to stand on hinge side of room 218's balcony door, and we waited.

Shortly we heard a knock on the room's interior door. Then came the voice of our newly hired friend. "Excuse me, Mr. Smith. The manager sent me. The sheriff is down at the front desk. He's asking to speak with you."

Near instantly we heard feet lightly hit the floor. Muffled sounds of dressing followed, and not quite so muffled curses from pain. A moment later the door eased open in front of us. Then the snout of a short-barreled revolver came into view.

I threw myself at the door with all the force I could muster. The door's edge slammed into the hand holding the pistol. The weapon flew down the balcony. The gun's owner ended up wedged between door and jamb with my weight fully on it. His hand darted for his trouser pocket. The butt of T.R.'s Colt slammed into that hand. Then his other hand smashed into the fellow's stomach. The last bit of fight went out of him.

We caused quite a stir as we marched our prisoner through the hotel lobby. Hands tied with curtain sash cord, he sported three self-applied plaster patches on his face, and a few others on his chest.

In the middle of the lobby he called out in a strong New York City accent, "Help me. I'm being kidnapped." The hotel's manager moved to step around the counter.

"Nonsense!" exclaimed T.R. "We are taking him to the sheriff by way of Dr. Marley's office for treatment of wounds received during his crime. He is suspected in an attempted murder. Anyone is welcome to accompany us, but interfere at your peril."

Mr. Bennett's driver collected our horses and followed us at some distance, keeping watch for trouble. A few minutes later we reached

Marley's Surgery again. Hardly had we entered when Miss Angela emerged from behind a curtain.

"That's him!" she exclaimed with veritable sparks shooting from her eyes. "If I still had that shotgun, I'd finish what I started." She then returned to Ashley's side.

"You got nothing on me!" exclaimed our prisoner.

"Quite the contrary," replied T.R. "My associates discovered that yesterday Hatchet Face Hogan was totally broke. He cadged liquor from all he met. This morning I took five Double-Eagle coins off his body. Brand new coins. I'll wager the sheriff can find out where you met him. Perhaps someone even saw you pass him the coins."

"You can't prove what I gave him, if anything," the fellow growled.

"Oh, but I think we can. For the coins bear the mark of the Philadelphia mint and are of 1892 manufacture. Many New Yorkers have not yet encountered this year's coins. In this territory new coins come from the mints of Carson City, Denver, or San Francisco. Only an Easterner like you could have given Hogan such mint fresh coins."

"And maybe you gave him the damned coins, you Wall Street Pretty Boy."

T.R. only smiled at the insult. "No, I think we can prove far differently. The late Mr. Hogan received the coins into greasy hands. He examined them carefully, probably because he did not trust you. Then he wrapped them tightly in a bandana and shoved that deep into his pocket. The prints of his fingers are still visible on them, and so, I suspect, are yours! In Great Britain, Sir Francis Galton has established a method for identifying what a criminal has touched by his unique fingerprints. You are lost. Be glad the charge will be only attempted murder."

The man fell silent. Then I spoke for the first time. I asked if he had been able to remove all the buckshot from his body. Before I could finish he flew into a rage.

"Another damn Limey! I'm sick of Limeys. Bad enough I work for one. Now fancy pants here wants to use one to lock me up and you want to cut me up. Dammit to hell all you Limeys!"

"Ah, so you do work for the Gentleman Dodger!" exclaimed T.R.

"Well played, this Roosevelt," commented Sherlock Holmes. "Very well played, using mint markings that most never notice to build his case. And fingerprints? Sir Francis' work has barely come into use, but your Mr. Roosevelt quotes him. An unusual man."

"T.R. bluffed in this case. Holmes. The prints of Hogan's fingers were apparent to all. But my friend had no idea how to make any other such visible. Still, it served for our purposes."

As the Dodger's name left Theodore Roosevelt's lips, our prisoner froze. Color drained from his face. I suppose a man realizing he had swallowed dynamite with a lit fuse would look as this fellow did.

"Wh... Where did you hear that name?" came his strangled whisper.

T.R. continued to bluff. "I am an official of the United States Government. You would be surprised what I know. The central government does not intervene in purely local criminal business. But you have crossed the borders of several sovereign states to perpetrate this act. That makes it a Federal affair."

The fellow looked even more crestfallen, if that is truly possible. He tried to speak, but could not form a coherent sentence. As he fell silent, T.R. pounced.

"Not much to say? I am not surprised. Soon we will take you to the sheriff. Word will get out soon enough about the New York gang member come to Deadwood for a killing, and I will be sure that the name of your employer reaches the press. The South Dakota Clarion will most surely send the story quickly to the New York Clarion, and that name will figure prominently in the dispatch.

"We saw a criminal New Yorker on a similar errand killed by his own colleague as soon as he was captured in the Adirondack Forest. A similar fate waits for you, I am certain. That fate will find you here in Deadwood, or in the state penitentiary should you be somewhat lucky.

"Or we could simply let you walk out of here, if you do not cooperate. Word will already be all over Deadwood. Ashley Morstan's saddle partners would sweep you up off the street long before you could reach the train station. What they would do to you shouldn't happen to a rabid dog."

With that, T.R. launched into a listing of lingering deaths worthy of any Dime Novel. When he recited what fire ants would do to a face covered in molasses, the man began to tremble, and T.R.'s examples of retribution only became worse after that. Within five minutes Bogart Oswald, for that was his name, agreed to help us in return for his life.

Here Dr. Marley helped us out. For it seemed that Winslow Howell, the well known town drunk and burglar, had died overnight while rifling the boudoir of the mistress of a very rich and very married man. Said rich man arranged for quiet disposal of the body via Dr. Marley.

"Ah, so you do work for the Gentleman Dodger!" exclaimed T.R.

And so it was that Bogart Oswald became Winslow Howell. He agreed to plead guilty to a recent burglary for which T.R. would use his influence to obtain a lenient sentence. Then Bogart Oswald, née Winslow Howell, would succumb to his wounds and be promptly buried.

The newly renamed Mr. Howell answered our questions for most of the afternoon. I filled three notebooks during the interrogation. Our questioning ended, we tied up "Mr. Howell." Miss Angela guarded him with Dr. Marley's fowling piece as we rode to the sheriff's office and town jail.

Sheriff Ben Carson—no relation to Kit Carson, he hastened to say— turned out to be very receptive to our plan. Not only did it take the ticklish Howell situation off his hands, it kept him from worrying about a further influx of New York troublemakers.

While we worked out the details, Mr. Wilson's man, Oliver, caught up with us to deliver our purchases and our train baggage. We changed clothing in the sheriff's quarters. I to my own garments and T.R. to new western-style togs that he could use again on his next westward trip. We returned the "slops" garments and the holsters. It was late afternoon as we prepared to leave.

As we walked out of the jailhouse, the sheriff remarked, "I sent word to Jenny's. She's the only one this side of the station with decent grub. Your dinner should be ready about the time you get there."

As we walked, I must admit, I took careful note of the locals and what they wore. Not nearly as many men wore "six-shooters" as I had been led to believe in such a place. Fancy holsters were even scarcer. But many holsters there were. I felt a bit out of place with my service revolver simply in my coat pocket. T.R., being very much a hunter, obviously favored a long gun. However, his Colt sat firmly in a well broken-in holster on his left side with the butt facing forward. T.R. being right handed, I believe this arrangement is referred to as a "cross-draw rig."

I was not surprised that a number of people stared after us. T.R. tended to stand out, no matter the location. And I? I must have seemed the quintessential newcomer or "dude" as is often said. I kept watch as you had endeavored to teach me, Holmes, but I detected nothing beyond idle curiosity and ill concealed mirth at our appearance as we led our horses down that street.

The cafe known as "Jenny's" sported a well-painted sign applied to very rough sawn boards, nearly raw timber. We crossed the dusty street to pass under the sign. Inside the tables were also rough hewn, but T.R. appraised them as well appointed for the region.

As our eyes adjusted to the interior, I turned to my companion, "Shall we inspect the kitchen, T.R.?"

"A capitol idea," he replied as we headed to the nearby kitchen door. "But don't be surprised at anything we encounter...."

As he spoke he pushed the door wide with his usual gusto. A word died in his throat. Surprised were we indeed. One man with a bright bandana covering his face held the kitchen staff at six-gun point. A tray with two fine looking meals set out on it lay on a large table. Standing over it another roughly dressed man with bandana mask shook some sort of powder over the food. Never for an instant did I believe the man sprinkled salt.

T.R. sucked in air to shout, "Hold on, here!" His hand darted for his holster.

I began to grope for my revolver, but with my other hand I snatched the heavy lid of a large kettle from a hook on the wall to my left. This I sailed sideways, but with some force, at the outlaw guarding the staff.

It was well that I did. The lid smashed into the side of the man's neck as he turned to aim at us. He staggered. His pistol wavered. Before he might recover, a huge cast iron skillet in the hand of the angry cook smashed his tall topped Stetson around his ears.

I gained a grip on my revolver as the man with the suspect powder drew his heavy pistol. An explosion sounded to my right as T.R.'s weapon fired. His aim true, the man's right shoulder showed first a burst of dust, then blood flowed as the man spun backwards.

With my revolver finally in hand, I noted the cook and waitresses flat on the floor. The cook jerked his head to the rear. "One more in the back," he hissed.

I ducked behind the end of the big stove. T.R. took his cover from a heavy butcher's block. In this case fortune favored the cautious. The final outlaw wore a double-rig, as they call it, and the two pistols from that rig blazed away at us. We both fired a couple of rounds in return. I leaned further around the edge of the stove. I saw the legs of the outlaw from beneath the table holding our meals. I fired. The bullet splintered the door frame he stood near. He leapt almost straight up, and he hit the wooden floor again moving fast.

The surviving outlaw fairly sprinted out the rear door of the kitchen. T.R. and I took care not to be shot as we emerged thereafter. We saw a trail of dust marking his escape by horseback over the hill behind the building. Our boots clattered on the wooden boardwalk as we hurried around to the front of the cafe.

We reached our horses. As we each grabbed for the reins, we both paused. We looked at each other, then simultaneously said, "Reload!"

Reload we did. Soon we left our own cloud of dust in the wake of the would-be poisoner. Our horses were fresh and of high quality. I clung tightly, as my experience upon a galloping horse was still minimal, and mostly with English tack instead of a cowboy's saddle and bridle.

We raced among the rolling hills of grass, and we seemed to be gaining. Finally we saw a rider ahead. The silver conchos around the crown of his Stetson flashed in the late afternoon sun. Again we looked at each other, this time with great satisfaction.

A moment later the outlaw swung his mount to the right. A low hill obscured our view for a moment. We rounded the hill to see his dust trail heading through a small draw in the hillside. Boulders lay scattered all around the area. We turned our horses toward the draw.

I thought I could see our prey in the distance when T.R. forced his horse across in front of mine. My steed shied. I clung to the saddle horn with all my might. Through the rushing sound of near panic in my ears, I heard Roosevelt shout, "*Ambush!*"

My frightened horse shuddered to a stop right next to a large chunk of granite. I dived from the creature's back to the cover of the rock. It is well I did. A bullet sang past my ear as I dove. My horse bolted.

I peered around the boulder, revolver in my hand. I could see nothing that moved.

"T.R.," I hissed.

"Here, Watson," came the low reply. "One of the rascals looked up a second too soon. Else we'd both be buzzard bait. I saw two behind rocks where the draw narrows. Has to be at least one, or more, on the ridges. Probably with rifles."

"Were you able to unsheathe your Winchester?" I asked.

"That I did, but little good it will do at the moment. The glasses I wore are broken, and my spare set lost the right lens as I dived for cover. I can't shoot worth one of your plugged Farthings with my left eye. Can you use the thing?"

"My use of a long gun is limited to target shooting with a point-two-two. Not sure I could control your weapon, but I can indeed see to use it. By the bye, why aren't they shooting at us?"

"We're giving them nothing to shoot at. Contrary to Buffalo Bill's Dime Novels, nobody sprays the air with precious ammunition without reason.

Someone may well try to work around behind us..."

At that point we heard a shout of rage from the top of the left hand hill. A man in denim scrambled to his feet and whirled to face away from us. We, that is I, could just make out another figure confronting the ambusher. The outlaw tried to draw his sidearm, but the newcomer struck before the pistol cleared leather, as they say out there. An incredible smash to the jaw sent the fiend tumbling down the steep and very rough hillside, hand still gripping his weapon.

The action happened so fast that I could not take in the looks of our rescuer. On the opposite hilltop another man rose to aim a Winchester at the newcomer. In a move so fast that my eye could not follow, our new friend drew a Colt Peacemaker and fired. The man on the opposite hill crumpled and lay still. It was only at that point that I realized that our rescuer wore a full face mask.

The man dropped from sight. A moment later he reappeared as he used a rope to slide safely down the nearly vertical hillside. A thick rawhide glove protected his left hand from the rope. His rock-steady right hand pointed his Peacemaker at the boulders nearby.

From behind those rocks we heard a terrified yell, "It's the Devil Dick himself!"

The man rose to aim at the descending figure. I snapped off a shot with my service revolver. The round smashed a chunk of rock off the boulder. The outlaw flinched as rock chips tore into his side. Then the masked man's Peacemaker spoke. The outlaw fell straight backwards over the boulder, never to move again.

The masked man let go of the rope as he pushed off from the side of the hill. A well-timed move it was, Holmes. Two shots hit the hill just behind where he slid the instant before. Without thinking for my own safety, I stood to see him hit the ground of the draw rolling. The Peacemaker roared once more. Then silence.

The masked man stood. He began to look around when T.R. shouted, "Look out!"

I could barely see that the bandit who had rolled down the hill, aiming at the back of our rescuer. T.R. emptied his revolver. I saw the villain jerk to the side as he yanked off a single shot. The masked man staggered and grasped his left arm.

A moment later T.R. kicked the gun form the outlaw's hand. Relieving the other fallen outlaw of his gun, he inquired, "Are you badly injured, sir?"

"Not too badly, I do believe," came the reply. "I am chagrined that I did not make sure of that ruffian. Thank you for remedying the matter. I take it, however, that your spectacles did not start life as a monocle"

"Indeed not, my friend," said T.R. with a bit of a chuckle, "but the monocle served almost well enough. I am sorry I was not a trifle faster to save you that wound."

"Had you been a trifle less accurate, that projectile would be introducing itself to my gall stones, instead of passing through my arm."

Finally finding my voice, I said, "I am a doctor, sir. Please let me treat you. Heavens, it's far the least I can do to repay your rescue of us."

The masked man hesitated. "You have experience with bullet wounds?"

"On the battlefields of Afghanistan, and a nick in that very area upon myself. I did not bleed nearly as much as you have. I fear there is fairly large vein open."

"Ah, an officer and a gentleman. And you stand by your oath not to speak about your patients?"

"If that is your wish. Of course I do not know exactly who I might be treating."

"Indeed," said he, "but you may say that you have met he who is known as Deadwood Dick."

As we spoke, T.R. reached his horse. A moment later he pressed a small medical kit into my hand. He made as to follow me to where Deadwood Dick now sat upon one of the boulders.

The masked man looked up sharply. "I fear, sir, that I must insist that you remain where you are."

T.R. simply nodded and said, "As you wish."

As I approached, I pulled out my pen-knife to cut away his sleeve.

"Doctor, I must request that you only open my shirt just enough to do your work, but not an inch further. You will perceive why in just a moment."

I slit the sleeve a few inches front and back. Then I produced a swab to cleanse the wound with alcohol. I pulled open the sleeve and drew in a sharp breath.

"Now you understand," whispered Deadwood Dick.

"Indeed I do, and your near Shakespearian speech also serves as a disguise?"

"Quite correct, Dr. Watson. You did learn a thing or two from Sherlock Holmes."

I continued the treatment. When finished, we offered him our thanks. He told us to confide our needs or suspicions in Mr. Stanley, the editor of the newly renamed South Dakota Clarion. He would hear of it.

"Now, Holmes, what can you deduce or surmise about Deadwood Dick?"

"There are a few, even if remote, possibilities. He might have had a distinctive tattoo, or even scar, in the immediate area of the wound. A deformity would be much less likely, as most such would be observed through all coverings but possibly a suit of armor.

"The most likely supposition would be that the fast shooting Mr. Dick is not white. Am I correct?"

"Indeed you are, Holmes. Deadwood Dick is a Negro. But I must ask you to keep that confidential."

"Of course, my dear fellow. Now, please, on with your amazing narrative."

By the time we returned to Deadwood, a beautiful sunset graced the sky around us. We reported the attack to Sheriff Carson without mentioning the assistance of the so-called Black Rider. The clearly astonished Carson agreed to send a party for the bodies the following morning. We sought hotel beds as soon as we assured ourselves that our prisoner was secretly in the hands of the sheriff's men.

Morning found us breakfasting privately with the judge of the local court. He agreed to our plan and wished us luck. He also hinted that he knew the true story of our gunfight at Lakota Draw, as the place was known. This statement came as a bit of a shock as we had not mentioned Deadwood Dick to a living soul, nor had we intended to do so. By the bye, Dr. Marley's assistant, ostensibly representing a charitable committee, arranged for the funeral necessary to our deception.

All else done, we proceeded to the offices and pressroom of the South Dakota Clarion. There we met Mr. Stanley, the editor and former publisher before Franklin Havens bought him out. His dark hair turned out to be far grayer at the temples than mine, but, he positively radiated energy. He led us to his office, but he had trouble closing the door for some printing supplies sitting in front it it.

"Gentlemen, that just shows you how seldom I need to have a private meeting," he began. "Now, I'm told that you met the Black Rider of the Black Hills yesterday."

T.R. and I looked at each other uneasily.

"Fear not, friends," continued Stanley. "None shall hear about it from me or the Clarion. Franklin Havens feels, as I do, that sometimes the law is best served by someone outside of it. Thankfully, there is little need of Deadwood Dick these days. Now how may I help you?"

We quickly explained our ruse. To our relief Mr. Stanley agreed to fully cooperate in the scheme. With our business concluded, he asked, "Does something trouble you, Dr. Watson? You look a bit ill at ease."

"To be frank, Mr. Stanley, I expected a considerable argument from you. What with your Constitution guaranteeing Freedom of the Press."

"You did well to come here, sir," he replied. "Had even a whiff of your plan come to me, we would have been after the story as you English are supposed to say 'foot, horse, and Marines.' Since I now understand that this is for the greater good, I am happy to cooperate."

"I am definitely glad you feel that way, sir," said T.R. "Some New York papers would print such a story just to sell a few extra papers. Like The Comet, for instance."

"Sometimes secrets need to be kept, Mr. Roosevelt. I am certain Dr. Watson sits on a few huge ones from his time spent with Sherlock Holmes. Some secrets do have a long shelf life, others need an eventual airing. At one time my very life, and possibly statehood for all the Dakotas, rested on keeping one secret about my own self. A cabal of power drunk men tried to prevent statehood until they controlled the entire Dakota territories. I fought them with the paper as best I could, but that was not enough. So I donned a mask. Today that is still not mentioned in public. But most old timers around here know that for about a year *I* took on the role of Deadwood Dick."

He did so with the original's blessing, I might add, Holmes. That revelation was the last surprise, good or bad, that we received in the Dakotas. Soon we headed eastward again. With the secret Morstan documents in our possession we took an even more circuitous route. The trip, while dull, proved uneventful. We detrained in a place called Hoboken, a city in the state of New Jersey. There we boarded a local line for New York City.

Arriving in the city, we received a message at the train station clearly intended for myself alone. That message directed us to an unprepossessing establishment with the unadvertised facility of a telephone. A very guarded telephone conversation sent us on the first of several quests. Finally, beneath a Chinese laundry, we were greeted by Detective Walter Brooks.

We poured out our story to him. Brooks kept a professional demeanor throughout our narrative, but I saw signs of excitement in his eyes when we described the involvement of illicit telegraphic information in our adventures.

When our recitation ended, Brooks called for the owner of the laundry. The two talked in mostly whispers. I decided that Brooks asked for some favor, or privilege, from the man. Apparently the fellow recognized T.R.'s name in a favorable light. When he looked again at me, Brooks spoke intensely. His voice thus carried just a bit more than before. The words "Sherlock Holmes" barely reached my ears. The Chinese looked up sharply. He asked the detective a question. Brooks nodded. The fellow hurried from the room. We heard his light footsteps on the stairs.

"We have been granted a very significant favor by our host," said Brooks with a sly smile. "We will leave here via tunnels few whites even dream exist. And far fewer have seen so much as a single entrance, much less traveled in them. There is, however, an unusual payment to be made for it. Ah, that was fast...."

The Chinese, in a traditional robe of a type I had also seen in London, came back into the room. I could see something behind his back as he stood in front of me and bowed politely. I returned the bow with no idea of his intentions.

"Dr. Watson," he said with little sign of the sing-song voice we heard when we entered his establishment, "please sign this."

With that he held out a book. I recognized not a single written character on the volume, for every bit was Chinese. As I took it into my hand I saw what his own hand had covered. For the cover of the book was decorated with a painting of the two of us, Holmes. To hide my astonishment, I flipped through the pages and found many of Sidney Paget's drawings, as well.

I bowed and said, "I would be honored to sign this. Thank you for your help."

A short time later a bullseye oil lantern in Brooks' hand gave just enough light to guide us through a positive maze of tunnels beneath the streets of New York.

We must have traveled a full mile before we exited to a grimy back alley. I looked questioningly at T.R. He had no more idea where we were than I did. With the lantern shielded, Brooks led us to a notch in a wall at the other end of the block. Here he pushed on a brick, then pulled on one of several metal rings. Another brick he slid over where the mortar was missing. His actions continued until I become sure he intended us not to know which actions actually caused a bricked-up door to silently swing open. Using the barest sliver of light from the lantern, he directed us to some old but serviceable chairs. We waited as he went to check on something.

"Gentlemen, I have considered what you have related and shown to me," said Brooks on his return. "For the time being I can not, and will not, trust the telegraph. There are telegraph keys and, more recently, telephones in our police stations. I shall also assume that even supposedly direct wires should not be trusted. Communication with my fellow officers and superiors must be in person, or not at all. Only the briefest of written messages will I dispatch, and those by some people I fully trust. While not all young, they operate in a manner similar to Mr. Holmes' Baker Street Irregulars. Now, I will bring you up to the current day regarding our own inquiries."

He led us up several flights of stairs. There he lit three lanterns revealing a sitting room full of comfortable, if slightly threadbare, furniture. As we made ourselves comfortable, he continued.

"My fellow officers followed the visitor to the Gentleman Dodger. They also intensified the watch on the Dodger. Any change in his actions was checked and double-checked. The information you brought back brings the Dodger's arrest and prosecution a gigantic step nearer. All of New York State will benefit from that moment.

"The Dodger's visitor, by a circuitous route, ended up near the docks. He entered a building called 'The Midlands,' which is owned by an English firm of the same name. The company is of fair reputation, if not a great deal of success in turning a profit in recent years.

"Along the way, a dwarf known as Tiny Tom tried to sell him a newspaper. Tom can look exactly like a five year old, if properly groomed. No one suspects him of being more than a potential pick-pocket. An hour later Tom presented me with this drawing of the individual. Quite an artist, our Tom."

Better than a camera for an active investigation, Holmes. For the fellow has what is fast becoming called a photographic memory. Couple that with a deft hand with pencil and brush, and soon a good likeness of a suspected criminal spreads across Manhattan Island like gossip shot from a cannon.

"When that man emerged again," Brooks continued. "He was followed to his lodgings. These were in a modestly prosperous neighborhood where questions about residents are not at all welcome. By the time the man reemerged next morning every watcher carried copies of Tom's drawing. For the next few days, all his actions beyond his quarters came under close scrutiny. Two nights later he returned to the Dodger's headquarters.

"Again the listeners could not hear many details, but they did hear him state that he had received new instructions. That caused consternation. For he had received no mail, no telegrams, no notes under his door, and no visits in the dockside business building where he apparently was the sole occupant, and there was no known telephone in any of these locations.

"The Dodger's right hand was soon dispatched on an errand. He proceeded to an infamous tavern that caters to the vilest, but most talented, criminals for hire. No police dared enter for fear of spooking the lot of the patrons. The fellow apparently talked briefly to several inhabitants of the place. Soon after he left, a few men drifted out into the night. We believe this included the two you encountered at Camp Liberty.

"With success of that mission reported to the Dodger, the visitor departed for his quarters. At that point I began to quietly check every city record concerning the visitor, his place of both lodging, and business. Little turned up. Far too little, in fact. Not even a building inspection for the last several years that did not read like the author had never entered the premises of either business or dwelling. Our City Engineer has the set of plans filed some thirty years ago by the builder. There are no notations on any part of them marked 'As Built,' and no record of inspections during the building survive. In this city, gentlemen, that smells. Smells to high heaven.

"Now, let me show you what details I possess. Any suggestions would be most welcome."

Smells, I thought. Smells. An idea began to form in my head.

"Brooks," I said some time later, "all your information indicates that little material enters or leaves these places. Does either building have public electricity? Or natural gas connections?"

He consulted a notebook before replying. "Both buildings have gas for lighting. A small gas plant is located in the northernmost building of the group containing the Midlands. Both buildings of interest burn coal for heat. The dwelling's block is not yet served by electricity. The business has electricity available, but is not known to be connected to the service. The Midlands once contained a large steam engine to run factory machinery long since removed. Therefore, the structure might provide its own electric power, at need. Do you have an idea, doctor?"

"The beginnings of one, Brooks. Could you have your Irregulars listen with a stethoscope at the walls, doors, coal chute, and so forth?"

"Not for very long," replied Brooks. "The businesses in that neighborhood formed an Association decades ago. They maintain private patrols of the entire area. Vagabonds and loiterers of all types get firmly moved along, and repeaters often face trespassing charges. Over the next day I can arrange for a few minutes listening in various places. No more that that."

"That should suffice, I think. And, if possible, include the nearby buildings. From your information, nothing larger than a solicitor's briefcase seems to go in and out of our target building. That eliminates a large percentage of criminal activity. Opium and most other smuggling requires a larger volume of material. So does counterfeiting. That leaves only a few possibilities," I concluded.

"Indeed it does," continued Brooks. "Unless clandestine methods to enter and exit that building are present. I will arrange what you wish as soon as is possible. And by your demeanor, I suspect you have another request or two."

"I've an idea for after we are in possession of more information. I am not quite sure of the American term, but I need to talk to someone who works in a chemical laboratory. Not what we British call a chemist, mind you. I think you call them 'druggists.' I mean more of a scientist."

***

As Brooks got the investigation into the Midlands Building started, he saw that I was escorted to a building on the Columbia College campus. Here I met Professor Stanford, one of his mentors. Stanford in turn introduced me to the head of the school's chemistry department. I explained my idea. The Chemistry Professor, knowing Brooks and his work, told me my needs could and would be addressed with great dispatch.

Again in a covered carriage, I returned to the run-down building serving as Brooks' temporary headquarters. The place stood a full story taller than any for blocks around. At full summer the place would be like a furnace, for very little air circulated with the windows boarded over. With nothing further to do, T.R. and I dragged cots onto the roof and slept nearly the clock around.

At mid-morning the following day the three of us met in an inner room of the second floor. Kerosene lanterns backed by polished metal reflectors studded the walls, making the entire area suitable for the closest work. Heavily used, but clean, desks, tables, and chairs filled much of the space.

"Good morning, gentlemen," said Brooks with a smile. "Breakfast, and a few other things, have just arrived. Please sit, while I serve. A working brunch for me."

With that Brooks removed the top of what I took to be a rubbish barrel. From the thing he pulled chaffing dishes and tableware. As T.R. and I served ourselves of the substantial plain-cooked food, the Detective removed stacks of papers, newspapers, reference books, and a locked box marked with the Columbia College seal. This he placed next to me.

As he served us coffee from a large vacuum bottle, he asked, "Aren't you anxious to open your package, Dr. Watson?"

"Not until we are long finished eating," I replied. "May I ask if your Irregulars were able to discover anything about the Midlands?"

Brooks paused to finish a bite of a baked egg dish I did not recognize. "Indeed they did. Though I am not sure what to make of some of their reports. As you know from the original plans, the Midlands contains a single, high ceiling floor with only a small cellar said to contain just the steam boiler and the remains of the machinery the boiler once drove. The factory floor was converted to offices some years ago. My Irregulars took turns listening at all parts of the building. They could not long tarry for the regular Association patrols. At all windows and doors, save the one used by Mr. Armbruster, they heard absolutely nothing. Behind that one door sounded 'open' or 'hollow' depending on the listener.

"They also listened at the walls of the basement and the coal chute. At places corresponding to the basement area, they heard a mysterious noise. They described the sound as a subdued but constant clicking or clattering. The sound seemed spread over much or all of the cellar area. In one corner they reported hearing the occasional voice above the unknown background sounds. And probably more than one voice. No words could be heard clearly enough to be transcribed."

I listened to Brooks while I glanced through a thick pile of incident reports turned in by those watching the Gentleman Dodger and Mr. Armbruster while T.R. and I sojourned in the Wild West. Then something caught my eye. I made a note on a pad of paper. Searching backward in time I made three other notes.

When Brooks finished his recital, I said, "Something seems to be odd here, Brooks. The covert search of Armbruster's lodgings included an inventory of his small larder. A tin of The Great Atlantic and Pacific Tea Company's finest China tea is listed, but no coffee. Nor is there any apparatus for brewing coffee listed. Yet, on the first day he was closely watched, he bought two pounds of very cheap coffee on the way to the Midlands Building. He repeated the purchase on the same day of each week we were gone.

"Yet the man is said to be the only person known to work in that building. Are we to assume he drinks a very fine and expensive tea while at home, but swills much low quality coffee as he works? I think not, sir. There is a good possibility, I believe, that some sort of staff secretly works in the Midlands, or in a building secretly connected to it. Or both, perhaps. And I'll wager that some of that staff works overnight there, as well."

"Thank you very much, Doctor," replied Brooks with a grin. "I thought I must be missing some things in that myriad of pages. Now you have put your finger directly on one such. Let us look at a map of the whole area."

Look we did. The Midlands lay in a two by three block area with several railroad tracks to either side of the structures. Along with the tracks, the business association protected and patrolled only these buildings. Brooks told us that he felt tunnels under the tracks would be dangerous in the extreme. Tunnels among the group of buildings seemed far more likely. Large numbers of people worked in more than one of the others. These, at the beginning and end of a normal business day, could be the entry and exit of a covert staff for the Midlands.

When we agreed on this possibility, I said, "I hope that the Professor's package holds enough to do the job."

"And what job might that be, Watson?" inquired T.R. with a look of anticipation on his face. Brooks' looked about the same.

I told them.

"A nice bit of work, Watson, sifting the coffee and tea business from the pile of chaff," commented Sherlock Holmes. "I must admit that I am curious about your mysterious package of chemicals. Has it something to do with illumination gas?"

"Indeed, Holmes. You will soon see," I replied as I stood over Mrs. Hudson's excellent smelling gooseberry pie at the sideboard. "Ah, this is now cooled just enough to slice. I shall continue as soon as we eaten our dessert. This next part of my tale might ruin our enjoyment of Mrs. Hudson's baking.

Detective Brooks demonstrated yet another skill once he put our combined plan into motion. Much as I hate doing so, I had written up my notes of the whole affair on the various trains we rode on our eastward march. These I dictated as Brooks fingers fairly flew on the keyboard of a Hammond model 1B typewriter. The machine, unlike all others I had previously encountered, made the paper visible during the typing.

In the early afternoon Judge Grover Hamilton of the highest city court arrived. T.R. and I were placed under oath by him. We told our stories as they related to matters within his jurisdiction. In his presence I signed the typewritten pages and T.R. attested to their correctness. His Honor, as the Americans address their judges, soon issued warrants relating to our plans for that night.

Then came the wait for darkness.

***

Our covered carriage stopped two blocks outside the railroad tracks that surrounded our target buildings in an eye-of-the-needle fashion. We were met by a uniformed police sergeant whose uniform remained for the moment under a light Inverness cape. Also there I recognized, in mufti—O'Brien—the stalwart officer from the disaster at Gio's establishment. Brooks spoke briefly with the sergeant. Then Officer O'Brien joined us as we slipped through the alleyways. We emerged at the closest point to the building housing the district's coal gasification plant.

Though warned by Brooks, T.R. and I almost drew our revolvers when a shadow detached itself from the shallow recess of a doorway. Horace, the only name given by Brooks, seemed even thinner than Mr. Wilson's ranch hand, Oliver. He nodded at the proper intervals as I instructed him in the use of the device the university prepared for me. With no questions, Horace fairly slithered across the tracks, well able to use telegraph and telephone poles for the fullest of cover.

The four of us, mindful of the Association patrols, took another tack to reach the target cluster of buildings. We paused one structure from the Midlands Building. The others took in the lay of the land. I used one of the unusual timepieces Brooks loaned to T.R. and myself.

You have seen watches constructed for the blind, Holmes. The crystals may be raised so the hour may be determined by touch. These Brooks adapted for clandestine work at night. The dial, case, and chain a matte coal black, the crystal then replaced with an opaque material that helped deaden the ticking. All being quiet, we approached the Midlands.

Earlier that afternoon I asked Brooks about the possibility of alarms of an electrical nature. After all somebody believed to be intercepting the contents of telegrams could well be expected to understand much of electricity. I listed the various items I had seen you and others use to detect and defeat traps of that nature. Brooks understood the principles already. He managed to assemble a kit containing most of the items I mentioned while himself adding a few more.

Using probes, tiny charged Leyden jars, and jeweled compass needles, we checked for electrical and mechanical alarms. We disabled the one that we found on the frame of the front door. Then Officer O'Brien produced an astounding assortment of lockpicks. With these he quickly turned both locks.

Slowly we pushed the door open enough for us to slip in. Information gleaned from honest delivery men and boys told us that Armbruster's public office lay just inside the vestibule. If he worked there now, all hope of surprise was lost.

Revolvers in hand, we advanced. A few gas flames behind protective glass gave barely enough light for us to inch forward. Armbruster's office: empty. Past there the corridor branched left and right. Out of sight from the street door, we found wooden crates—hundreds of them—stacked man high or higher in every office off of the corridors. Crates lined the corridor itself; Most had their lids attached by nails. They seemed full, but of something light. No wonder our listeners heard nothing. The crates served a secondary purpose as sound deadeners. We explored the corridor to the north, and found nothing but crates and more crates.

Suddenly we heard a heavy door slam open. The four of us sought cover in crate-packed offices. Peering out at ground level, I saw a man step into the far area of the south corridor. He carried a huge wicker basket brimming with some sort of material that appeared to be light and fluffy. He walked up to an open crate. With little wasted motion he emptied the basket into the crate, then shoved errant material inside. He picked up a block of something very dark from a sack nearby. This he added to the crate before nailing down the lid. He then retrieved the basket to walk back to the end of the corridor. Here he paused, doing something I could not at that time fathom. Holding the basket again he vanished. This time we barely heard the same door open and close as he left.

We waited for a minute or two, then advanced. We paused by the crate the fellow had closed. T.R. reached into the sack on the floor. From it he produced a large chunk of solid pitch. I'm sure we all shuddered. Whatever this building held in such quantity, any fire here would soon be a regional inferno like the Great Fires of London and Chicago.

Further down the corridor, and carefully isolated from the dangerous crates we discovered a firmly anchored table with a tiny fixed gas heating apparatus. On the thing sat a large percolator-type coffee pot. Here also sat the bag of cheap coffee purchased regularly by Mr. Armbruster. Cans of condensed milk and a large sugar caddy completed the service. A heavy

We explored the corridor to the north, and found nothing but crates and more crates.

door marked as "Blocked" stood in the nearby wall.

Cautiously we listened at the door. For the first time we heard a distant hint of the muffled clattering described by the Irregulars. A tiny amount of light came from under the door. Brooks slid a small mirror such as a dentist might use beneath the portal. Placing his eye to the ground, he moved the mirror's handle to its full extension, twirling it this way and that.

"A downward staircase. Enclosed. Looks just like the original building plans," he whispered. Finding no apparent alarms, we prepared to open the door. "Dr. Watson, how much time have we?"

I consulted the watch again. "A scant five minutes," I replied.

Under cover of his coat, Brooks lit a tiny bullseye lantern and quickly closed off all hint of its light. Silently we eased the door open. The badly lit enclosed stairs bore away to the right then, after a small landing, reversed course to descend further. Only a single wire-covered gas jet at the landing served to somewhat disperse the darkness. We eased down the stairs, T.R. and I on one side with Brooks and Officer O'Brien on the other. Past the landing a familiar flickering told us that the former boiler room used gas for light, rather than arc lights, lime lighting, or the new incandescent light bulbs.

As we approached the final steps, the clicking noise became more and more pronounced. An old and rough wooden door with a small inset window provided a view into the boiler room. But much light streamed through the glass, enough so that even the briefest look through the pane threatened our discovery. But light also intruded from several cracks between the boards of the door.

Brooks produced the small viewing device we are both familiar with, Holmes. In America they call it "the blackmailer's best friend." The pencil lead thick tube easily slid through the gaps in the wood. We took turns observing the lens-distorted panorama of the former boiler room.

What we saw reminded me no little of a model of a city. For nearly the whole of the former boiler room was filled with tables representing street blocks holding many near identical glass domed buildings. Narrow isles between the tables represented the streets. Along those streets walked six giants watching over the structures, and there must have been far in excess of one hundred of these glass "buildings."

Gaslight fixtures studded the walls. A half dozen chandelier fixtures provided a good level of light to the center area. Now and then the "giants," really men of course, would pause at one of the glass domes. Their hands would move as if observing some invisible thing held between them. Then the man would move to another dome to repeat the process. All the while the clattering waxed and waned like a never still ocean beach.

I felt of my pocket watch again. In less than a minute, Horace would release the chemical concoction. With the amount of gas consumed by the room's fixtures, the effect would quickly be apparent. Again I applied my eye to the viewing device.

One of the men stopped at a glass dome very near our door. This time I could see that he examined a strip of paper. In a flash I understood the place's purpose. Under each of the glass domes lay a telegraph printer or "ticker." That explained the clattering noise. Now the man tore off a section of the ticker's tape. I watched as he hurried to the back of the room. On a tall lectern he picked up a telegrapher's pasting device. Inserting the ticker tape, he affixed and cut the tape to fit a telegram form. Message completed, he placed the paper in one of a series of trays of which I estimated there to be more than fifty. Task completed, the fellow stretched his arms above his head. In that instant I saw a medium-sized pistol holstered under his left arm.

"They are armed," I hissed to my companions.

As T.R. took a turn viewing, I checked my service revolver yet again. Meanwhile Officer O'Brien began to examine the wall facing the bottom of the staircase. The plans for the Midlands indicated the existence of a service area for pipes from the former factory floor, and a connection to some sort of drainage system. Brooks' research told us that before the City built storm drainage culverts that this area would often be covered by standing water of up to a foot's depth. We hoped to take cover in that service area.

My next check of my watch told me Horace should have released the chemicals into the gas lines over a minute ago. Just as I whispered this to my companions, O'Brien quietly wrestled loose a section of the wooden wall. Brooks opened the bullseye lantern a tiny fraction while T.R. spread his coat to block any reflected light. For a moment all I could see were cobwebs. Then, dimly, I made out some space beyond. O'Brien produced a truncheon far longer that his issue nightstick. He twirled the thing to collect a large wad of webbing. Now we saw a man-high area extending some ten feet before dropping off into nothing. Two or three mice and rats scurried from view as the light increased.

The others ducked into the service area as I took a final look into the ticker room. The men still roamed the aisles. Then one stopped. His face took on a suspicious look. Then a man twenty feet away did the same. I retrieved the viewing device before I scrambled in with the others. Officer O'Brien pulled the section of the wall back into place behind me.

We waited.

"Have you an idea what we waited for?" I asked Sherlock Holmes as I refilled my after dinner pipe.

The great detective paused for a brief moment. "By your narrative, Watson, the men smelled something unusual. Illumination gas has no discernible odor. What you introduced into the gas system could not be dangerous or even sleep inducing, and most such would be consumed by passing through the flame of the fixtures. You and your companions neither fear the smell, nor do you seem to carry a defense against this chemical. I must conclude the object is to induce some action by causing fear."

"Fear indeed, Holmes," I replied. "As usual you have the right of it. Poison mine gas often carries the smell of hydrogen sulfide. Most people today associate that smell with danger of one kind or another. Professor Thurston and his colleagues contrived a compound that carried that smell and survived the burning of the illumination gas. We hoped to hide until after the ticker men evacuated the place. Failing that, we would storm in while the blighters were disoriented. And it worked. For suddenly every ticker machine fell silent."

The silence seemed deafening. Ears to the wall into the ticker room we heard running sounds. A voice called out, "All out, lads. If the smell's in the Baker Building, we rally at the track crossing!"

We waited two full minutes after the last sound from that room faded into silence. We then emerged into the stairwell. The ticker room lay mostly dark. Only a few wire-covered gaslights of the mine safety variety remained lit. After a brief observation we pushed open the door and entered.

A quick search proved the room truly empty of occupants. Somehow we managed to ignore the sickening smell of hydrogen sulfide. Brooks posted Officer O'Brien at the exit tunnel we found leading from the far wall. T.R. and I removed small coal oil lanterns from the cases we carried and got them alight. We began to search. Affixed to the wall next to the tunnel was a large slate chalkboard. On it were inscribed lists of words and phrases. Some were names of various government bureaus. Some were important men and their businesses. Gold and silver were there, and any number of other precious materials. Obviously some of the terms were changed from time to time. A few, such as the American Secret Service, had never been altered, and among such was the name "Morstan." In the more recent entries I discovered both our names, Holmes, but your brother's seemed to have been there far longer. In the most recent listing we found both "Theodore Roosevelt" and "Camp Liberty."

"Gentlemen, look here," called Brooks from a large desk. "Notes in Mr. Armbruster's hand. At least one is about locating the two of you. There are code books for American bankers' code plus many others, and cipher wheels and other devices I do not recognize. This is far larger an operation than I feared."

Brooks and T.R. fell to searching the desk drawers while I felt drawn to the trays containing the copied telegrams. I found them grouped by categories. Under railroads were trays for the Union Pacific, the Central Pacific, and so on. Then a tray marked "All Other RRs." Finally came an area of miscellaneous subjects. A recently altered label caught my eye. Where "Morstan" once stood alone, now the slip of paper said "Morstan, Watson, Roosevelt, Camp Liberty."

I pocketed the slips in that tray. Soon I discovered a group of trays devoted to Her Majesty's government. As I began to clean them out, a hand fell on my shoulder.

T.R. whispered, "Leave a few in each tray, Watson. Once word gets around, there will be an accounting. Empty trays will point straight to you."

Excellent advice from a true friend. I spent the next few minutes sorting out innocuous bits of information to leave behind. I suspect that Brooks also realized what I did, but he never gave me so much as a hint.

Behind the desk, a wooden wall hid various mechanisms. The group's leader pulled open a large three-bladed electrical switch to shut off the tickers and the machines that fed them. Next to that lay a switch of but a single blade. That device, by dust markings, seemed to always be open, but now it lay closed. Brooks commented that the thing's position might foretell trouble.

Brooks had the right of it, Holmes. T.R. later pieced together the consequences of that switch and informed me. Not long after the scheduled dumping of the chemical, the watchers at Armbruster's rooming house chanced to observe the cook of a tiny all night eatery dash from his establishment and into the alley where Armbruster's windows faced. He began tossing pebbles at those windows.

In a trice Armbruster's face appeared as he yanked open the sash. The cook spoke no more than two or three words, then departed. The window slammed shut before the cook took his first step. Soon the cellar door opened. Armbruster carried a bicycle up the short flight of stairs to the street. An instant later he peddled furiously in the direction of the Midlands.

***

O fficer O'Brien stood watch within the tunnel to the Midlands Building. Only a tiny amount of light came around the door. There he strained his acute senses for many minutes seeking any indication of the return of the crew of the infernal place. For a time all he heard were the scratchings of tiny rodent feet. Then came other faint sounds. At first he believed he was hearing things. Then the sounds came again. Bird sounds!

O'Brien slipped through the door. He found the three of us inspecting the devices that fed the ticker machines.

"Sir, please don't think I've gone daft. I hear birds out in the tunnel."

To say that the man received our complete attention is a vast understatement. We three looked at O'Brien, then each other.

"I always knew we dealt with smart men," said Brooks.

"Aye, infernally smart," growled T.R. as he slipped his Colt from its holster.

"Prepared for almost anything," said I. "We gave them the illusion of poison gas. They counter with canaries. Do we retreat, or take them on? I, for one, am tired of defensive actions."

"And I," spat T.R. as he clenched his free hand into a fist.

Brooks looked at us for the briefest of moments, to take our measure, I believe. "Best to catch them now, than to chase faces we are not sure of. And, with the money behind this, they may well have a duplicate of all this hidden away. Let us hide and confront them."

I soon selected a ticker table and crawled under it. From there I could aim for the legs of any man coming through the tunnel door. T.R. and O'Brien placed themselves far to either side of me setting up a nasty cross-fire situation. Brooks hid behind the desk, thus blocking a possible retreat if all of the men fully entered the room. We were truly ready. Or so we thought.

Then I looked up. My heart jumped to my mouth. Clamped on the underside of the table I saw a stick of dynamite! From my Army experience, I perceived it to be electrically primed and ready for detonation. The wire ran from the stick to a table leg and thence into the floor. In an instant I applied my pen-knife to the wire. As soon at the thing parted I scrambled to the next table. Only to find the same thing!

I pulled myself to an aisle and stood. "There is dynamite under the tables!" I hissed. "Quickly, cut the fuses."

T.R. pulled a sheaf knife from the top of his boot. Brooks flicked open a large folding knife. I passed my pen-knife to O'Brien as I took his place at the door. I no longer smelled the chemicals, but I felt sure that what stench remained only increased as the criminals approached. If they valued their lives at all they would advance but slowly, keeping a close eye on whatever birds they carried to detect a true menace.

At first I only heard the occasional chirp and twitter to be expected from canaries at rest. Then, still faintly, came the flutter of wings followed by the sound of hard boot soles on the brick tunnel floor. The birds settled as the party paused again.

The acoustics of that stopping place must have been in tune with my position. I heard a brief exchange of voices.

"The canaries show no distress."

"No. This will be our last pause. The devil alone knows what messages we've missed because of this. Come on now!"

I fairly slithered back inside. "They come," I whispered. "They enter with intent to start everything running again. Did you disarm all the explosives?"

"We believe so," replied T.R. "Including six sticks within the electrical box, and four more in the desk. Back to cover all!"

I shuddered as I resumed my position. The detonation of but a single stick in that confined room would likely burst the ear drums of all inside the doors. If not far worse.

In the eerie silence we clearly heard the approaching footsteps. The door swung open. I watched seven sets of legs enter.

A commanding voice said, "Tom, throw the power switch."

One set of legs detached itself from the others in the direction of the desk and power room. The canaries twittered as their cage was placed atop the desk. Then I heard a dull thud followed by the sound of Tom's collapsing body. All feet suddenly pointed in that direction, to my left.

From my right, Officer O'Brien bellowed, "Stop where you are! You are under arrest!"

For the slightest fraction of a second every foot I observed froze in place. Feet began to swivel from left to right. Hands reached for pants pockets.

"Stand fast or we open fire!" cried T.R. from my right.

One set of legs that pointed straight at me folded frog-like into a squat. Then the man dived under the table. He looked up as he pulled a pistol from the back of his waistband. His eyes went wide as he took note of me, and more importantly, the muzzle of my service revolver. His hand continued to move his weapon forward as I squeezed the trigger.

The room echoed like a thunderclap as my round took the man between the eyes.

Suddenly gunfire sounded from all sides. T.R. and O'Brien fired at men brandishing a pistol and a knife. Both men reeled. I watched their feet dance in front of me. The one with the pistol discharged a round as he fell. I heard the bullet whine off the stone wall. Then came the sound of much breaking glass as the projectile plowed through a series of ticker domes.

Brooks, I later discovered, simultaneously creased the skull of a third man trying to unload his pocket.

"Armbruster!" cried Brooks from behind the remaining group, "You are surrounded. Empty your hands. Now! Or die!"

I saw a pistol clatter to the floor. Then another. The three uninjured felons stood fast as O'Brien disarmed them and applied shackles. The battle was over, but—I feared—not the war.

***

First Brooks' Captain arrived. He immediately sent for the Chief of Police. On hearing an explanation about compromised communications and civilians being unavoidably involved, the Chief sent for members of the United States Secret Service. At this point T.R. informed the Chief that he, as a representative of the Federal Government, had brought the situation to his Department's attention.

This precipitated a round-robin discussion about what to do with the room and its contents. I cast about for a place to sit down. I feared the talking would continue for hours. As I turned, I found Officer O'Brien standing next to me.

With a crooked smile on his face, he said, "Now's the time for you to hot foot it outta here, Doctor. Mr. Brooks an' Mr. Roosevelt both feel you can do without all the palaver. Follow me, quietly."

We silently edged away from the discussions as they grew more animated. Once in the stairwell to the Midlands we hurried back onto the streets and through the police lines. O'Brien soon handed me over to Horace, who now drove a dilapidated salvage wagon drawn by two horses apparently requisitioned from a glue factory.

As we set off, Horace said, "Mr. Brooks thought you might like to pay a courtesy call on the British Council. Or we can go direct to the railway station. Your choice, Dr. Watson."

I changed clothing in the interior of the surprisingly quiet wagon. A gimbaled lantern and mirror allowed me to remove the burned cork from my face. I looked almost like an English Gentleman again as I clambered to the top of the wagon. From that perch I jumped over the fence of the residence of Sir Albert Prentice, British Counsel General for the City and State of New York.

A moment later I pounded on the door of the servants' entrance to the large dwelling. Shortly some light filtered from under the door. Then a head wearing a stocking cap appeared through a crack-like opening of the portal. I apologized for the late hour and assured the man that I was not drunk. Then I asked to see Sir Albert on a most urgent matter.

Still foggy with sleep, the poor fellow began to tell me to go to the Counselor Offices during business hours. His sleepy, but icily polite, speech unknowingly told me that the man had been born a Cockney. Recalling your lecture to Professor Higgins' Linguistics class, I used Cockney rhyming slang to inform him that I was prepared to raise Old Scratch himself to see Sir Albert.

His eyes opened wide. He inquired my name. His eyes opened yet wider.

"Yes, *that* Dr. Watson," I continued with a rueful smile. "Please give this paper to Sir Albert. If he does not faint dead away, he will see me at once."

The man took the paper and closed the door. I had given him a coded telegram sent the day before to England by Sir Albert himself. Glued to the back was the decoded version. In it Sir Albert made a very undiplomatic reference to Mr. James G. Blaine, the American Secretary of State. Three stories above me, a light came on. No words reached my ears, but I heard the irritable tones of speech. Then a sharp exclamation.

Seconds later the staff member reappeared, a crooked grin nearly split his face. He winked at me before whispering, "Gor Blimey, Gov'ner, I think he almost did keel over. I'm the one who gets to burn all such from this house. You have surely put the old fox in the henhouse, you have." In a normal tone he continued, "Please follow me, sir."

I spent about an hour with Sir Austin. He would have kept me there indefinitely, I think, but I made it clear to him that concerns for family safety trumped his need to ask the same questions yet again. Without his office staff ranged behind him, I believe he decided that his personal safety might be at risk should he try to detain me. And rightly so. Therefore, the fellow from the sound of Bow's Bells walked with me to where Horace waited, and I boarded the first train of the day for the Adirondacks.

I rented a horse at Saratoga Springs and struck out for Warrensburg. On a much warmer day than before, I made good time. The now fully leafed forest felt near church-like, almost as though being in a huge monument to the Good Lord's creativity. The old man at the stable called me by name as I entered. He told me that Mrs. Sanders, the governess, would likely be down a certain trail with her charges at this time.

Indeed she was, guiding the play of several youngsters in a clearing. I watched from the trail as she ended a game to let free play begin. One of the little girls saw me and waved. Mary noticed the girl's action as I waved back. She turned in my direction. An instant later she threw herself onto me with almost the verve of a Rugby player.

Not long after breakfast two days later, three coaches arrived at Camp Liberty. Banners—whose paint still smudged at a heavy touch—proclaimed those conveyed to be members of the well known English Physical Culture Society. Nathan informed me that the group rented a set of the simplest cabins owned by the camp, those being far from the main area. Soon much activity could be heard from that area.

Before my suspicions could grow further, two men from the group sought me out. To my satisfaction they identified themselves as Commander Renwick of the Royal Navy and Lieutenant Hurricane of the Royal Marines attached to our embassy. Letters from both Sir Albert and our Ambassador in Washington informed me that the "Culture Society" would see to Mary's and my safety until London was heard from.

It seemed that the H.M.S. Invincible had been coaling at the city of Boston. Every man aboard with any wilderness experience, from the lowest seaman to senior warrant, suddenly found themselves headed for Camp Liberty. I was requested to recount my experiences in detail to Renwick. The massive Lt. Hurricane would see to our safety.

There followed about three mostly enjoyable weeks. Whilst Mary cared for the children of the guests, Renwick and I would wander the trails seeking private places to talk. But one certain morning we found our destination already occupied. The small clearing held a break in the trees allowing one to see for miles. Two people stood in silence, taking in the view. Then the man placed his hand on the shoulder of the woman. She turned to face him, a slight look of hope, or perhaps anticipation, on her face. Renwick and I froze in our tracks. A moment later we saw Thaddeus Radcliffe kneel before Ester Gordon. Seconds later he rose to take her in his arms. As we quietly retreated, I am sure Renwick also noticed tears in both their eyes.

During this time I also received visitors. One of T.R.'s retainers made the trip twice with letters from his employer. Then one day Horace, of all people, sought me out. A huge grin endangered the proper location of his jaw as he handed over a folder from Detective Brooks. The letter on top proclaimed that the Gentleman Dodger now called New York City's prison farm his home. Information provided by T.R. and myself—coupled with data found in the ticker room—insured deportation as the absolute minimum to happen to the criminal boss.

Three days after that revelation, the Military Attache from our Embassy arrived in mufti at Camp Liberty. With him came a formal request, countersigned by your brother Mycroft, that Mary and I leave for England immediately.

And that is nearly the end of the story, Holmes. Commander Renwick joined us as we secretly boarded the Invincible. We made a near record crossing. I spent the better part of a month answering yet more questions. When the questions ended, I wanted to pursue the evidence described in the Morstan papers, and thence find out which of those four damnable families were responsible for our problems in America.

At that point our government, in the form of Mycroft Holmes, intervened. I was asked—instructed, is more like it—to wait six months before stirring those waters, and to speak to no one about the four families in detail. That is why I have omitted the contents of the Morstan patriarch's letter from my narrative. I thought about ignoring the request, but at about the same time Mary became sick. Since the time I lost her, I had been going through the motions of living... until you returned from the dead, my friend.

"That six months will soon be up, Holmes. Will you help me uncover whatever has them attacking the Morstans when generations have passed?"

"I shall speak with Mycroft tomorrow, Watson. Any who think of the Magna Carta—as they seem to—deserve to be discommoded at the earliest possible moment. This should be challenge enough to shake off my doldrums."

I answered a few minor questions about my story. Then I asked Holmes for the use of his kit of burglar tools. Moments later I carefully pried off the lid of T.R.'s crate. I removed padding made of raffia fiber and wadded newspaper.

Holmes spread out the first newspaper wad to find the front page of the New York Comet. He gave a rare chuckle. "Your friend has written across the masthead 'Watson, the only proper use for this publication, won't you agree?'"

The top layer contained a few knick-nacks and mementos of New York City, the Adirondack Park, Chicago, and Deadwood. With them was a fine pewter replica of the Statue of Liberty.

Next came a small folio holding many newspaper clippings related to the publicly known portions of our adventures. Between that and a larger folio I found a thin book on the history of the Amish people. The larger folio contained several sealed letters and the new years' brochure for Camp Liberty. Carefully wrapped with them I found two photographic prints. The first depicted the wedding party for the nuptials of Mrs. Ester Morstan Gordon and Brother Thaddeus Radcliffe. The other was the engagement picture of Miss Angela Wilson and Mr. Ashley Morstan.

Yet another package lay at the crate's bottom. About the size of a copy of The Strand Magazine, it yielded two canvasses. As the first was revealed Holmes and I both broke out laughing. The piece was executed in highly detailed pen and ink, with beautiful water colors bringing life to the scene. A facsimile of the engraved masthead for Beadle's Half-Dime Library filled the top. In the scene below, Theodore Roosevelt and I stood back to back in the midst of a Deadwood street. Dressed in our ramshackle borrowed western attire we exchanged gunfire with an assortment of desperadoes all around. A purported story title ran beneath our feet. It read: "Eastern and English Justice in Deadwood, or The Deadly Dudes." The line "by Ashley Morstan" completed the piece.

A note on the wrapping of the other canvas stated, "Based on photographs taken at Camp Liberty. I hope I have done her justice. Your friend and admirer, Ashley Morstan." I am not ashamed to say that the picture inside brought tears to my eyes. In the foreground my beloved Mary played with a group of children. The background appeared for all the world like a carved cameo of her smiling profile. Ashley did her more than justice. Holmes excused himself whilst I regained my composure.

My tale finished and the content of the crate revealed, Holmes reentered the room. He strolled to a side table to collect glasses and a decanter of port. Automatically he glanced out the window to Baker Street.

"I am not yet used, Watson, to passing these windows without worrying about something coming through them. Tonight I see a man loitering on the far sidewalk. An American by his clothing. All else appears normal."

He returned with another quick glance. "Apparently, he saw me. He now approaches our front door. As it is a bit late for callers, I suggest we go out and listen should he seek entry from Mrs. Hudson."

A moment later we did indeed hear Mrs. Hudson inquire as to the man's business. The clatter of a hansom cab covered the first few words of the reply. As the noise faded we heard the voice that was indeed American, and one familiar to me.

"... know that I have no legal standing, but I am here on official business to see Mr. Sherlock Holmes."

I kept my voice below a whisper, "I believe I know that voice, Holmes."

"Mrs. Hudson," cried Holmes, "send the gentleman up."

With that we retreated back into the rooms. A moment later Mrs. Hudson escorted our visitor to the door. He looked about as his eyes adjusted to the brighter light. I smiled. My ears had not betrayed me. Strange as it seemed, before us stood Walter Brooks of the Police of New York.

As he saw me, all his hesitant behavior vanished. "Dr. Watson," said he, "it is so good to see you again. And this must be the crate that preceded me across the Atlantic."

"And it is quite a pleasant surprise to see you here in London, Brooks," I said as we shook hands. "May I present to you Mr. Sherlock Holmes. Holmes, this is Detective Walter Brooks of whom I was telling you earlier this evening."

"Watson speaks highly of you, Detective," said Holmes cordially. "You apparently apply my methods where you can. I am flattered."

"Thank you, sir," replied Brooks as his grin threatened to split his face. "It is because of your methods, and Dr. Watson's assistance that I must now correct you. For I am now Detective Sergeant Brooks, and much of that promotion I owe to the two of you."

Before I could say anything, Holmes offered port for a toast to Brooks' promotion. Few police had I ever met so deserving. A moment later we eased ourselves into chairs.

I inquired, "What brings you to London, Brooks?"

"As a Sergeant, I became eligible for extradition work, Doctor. I've been to Cuba and Nova Scotia with a senior man. Then I came up for London for my first lone mission: A bank manager who bolted with a trunk full of cash not his own. He'll be no problem getting home.

"But as I waited at the docks to embark, an amazing thing happened. Frankly, I still pinch myself to be sure I did not dream the whole event. The first and second class passengers had boarded the steamer. Much of the waiting area stood empty, and well that it did.

"Just as the purser began to call for my third-class group, we all heard the clattering of horses' hooves on the cobblestones. And these were not the hooves of draft animals, but of a riding horse at a full gallop. A moment later, between the top of the low fence and the awning above, I could make out the horse's body. Coming fast was he, and I recognized what I could see of his tack as police issue. But the rider wore a suit of fine civilian clothing.

"Then the pair passed the entry vestibule to come alongside the un-topped portion of the fence. To my further amazement, the rider urged the horse into a jump. Over the fence they sailed. The rider stayed low on the creature's neck as the horse found his footing. I lost full sight of them behind a wide sign as the rider dismounted. Then a strident voice began shouting my name.

"I began to believe one of my old collars had bolted an asylum to seek revenge. Then I got sight of the man: None other than the newest member of the Police Commission of New York, Mr. Theodore Roosevelt!"

"The man seems truly amazing," exclaimed Holmes.

"I told you that you had no idea, old friend," I returned. "T.R. is nothing, if not surprising."

"Surprising is far too mild a word, Doctor," Brooks replied with a broad smile. "I ducked under a guide rope and approached as Mr. Roosevelt calmed the horse and thanked the steed profusely. I bid him good day and the amazing story poured out of him.

"'Sergeant Brooks, what a delightful irony,' he told me. 'That you, of all members of the force, should be sailing for London on this wonderful day. He's alive!'

"'Who is alive?' I asked. I felt completely as sea, so to speak, at that moment.

"'This might be the most storied return of a man from the grave since the Biblical Lazarus. I have just confirmed it by cable from Inspector Lestrade himself. Sherlock Holmes is alive!'

"In my astonishment I let out such a holler that I nigh on spooked the poor horse. Then I managed to thank him for the news and inquire about his near break-neck ride to the docks.

"He replied, 'Just two days ago I sent a crate to Dr. Watson full of mementos of our time together. Had I known of Holmes' return I would surely have included something for him. We never would have met Watson without his knowing Holmes. Therefore, I have a mission for you, Detective-Sergeant Brooks. To be carried out just as soon as your original assignment permits....'"

Brooks arose. From his inside coat pocket he pulled a rectangular packet carefully wrapped in thick waxed paper. He untied the string holding the paper to reveal a thin leather case.

"Mr. Holmes, in the name of the Police Commission of the City of New York, it is my honor, and distinct pleasure, to present to you these credentials. They name you an Honorary Member of the Police Force of New York, with the rank of Inspector of Detectives."

In all the years I knew Sherlock Holmes I could count the times I found him speechless on the fingers of one hand. This was one such occasion.

Watson on the Hudson
&
Other Places

I first encountered Sherlock Holmes via the early 1950s radio dramas. Basil Rathbone seemed like "the" Holmes for some decades. Nigel Bruce did a great job *on the radio* where the character generally received much better treatment than in film up to that time. I've since watched and listened to many actors as Holmes and Watson.

About thirty years ago I reviewed Loren D. Estleman's novel *Dr. Jekyll and Mr. Holmes*. I strongly agreed with Estleman's comments that the character of Dr. Watson suffered from near criminal mistreatment at the hands of various movie studios. Then many others based their adaptations on the resultant "comedy-relief" buffoon in so many films.

Poppycock! Watson is a competent doctor of medicine, for pity's sake. He survived being wounded in battle in Afghanistan, of all places. Don't sell him short. Holmes didn't. And I tried not to.

Then came Airship 27's anthology, *Sherlock Holmes, Consulting Detective*. I thought I'd hit it big with an idea for Dr. John H. Watson, late of Her Majesty's Fifth Northumberland Fusileers. (But Ron Fortier already had a different idea.) With Sherlock Holmes thought dead, New York Police Commission member Theodore Roosevelt would invite Watson to lecture on Holmes' methods to New York's Finest. And he would get involved in a few exciting cases. I would write the opening and first case. Other Airship 27 writers would fill the middle of the book. Then I'd close out the anthology with Watson solving a locked stateroom mystery on the voyage home.

I pitched the idea to Ron not knowing he already had *A Season of Madness*, the first Dr. Watson short novel by Aaron Smith, in hand. He didn't really want to do a Watson anthology. To top that off, I found that Roosevelt did not become a Police Commissioner until about the time Sherlock Holmes returned from the grave. Ron wasn't interested in trying any Imaginary or What If stories, either. Can't say I blame him.

But he was interested in another Watson short novel. Well, I thought, perhaps meeting Dr. Watson made T.R. more interested in that Commission opening. (The single position of *The* Police Commissioner did not come about until much later.) So, I'd be writing not about 15,000 words, but over 44,000. Second longest piece I've ever written.

Having Watson narrate the tale seemed a given. That's the format of the vast majority of the original stories. But I could not totally leave out Sherlock Holmes. Immediately the idea of Watson spinning the yarn to Holmes came to mind. And the semi-mysterious crate popped up about as quick. The Marstan family connection followed soon after. So I made notes. Gathered research. And started writing key scenes.

As I wrote the characters' dialog I tried imagining their voices. I heard Watson as a mixture of the two actors on the Granada Television series with bits of a younger Nigel Bruce. But I only heard one voice for the First Consulting Detective: Jeremy Brett!

At one point I thought Watson might finish in the United States and return to England to follow the Marstan mystery. I even selected the hero of "The Prisoner of Zenda" to assist him. Didn't happen. Maybe some other time.

Some random notes:

I've sprinkled the story with odd and obscure references and "hat tips." Some are modestly obvious. (The "Bar 20" ranch of Hopalong Cassidy, for instance.) Others mean little to anyone but myself. (The "S Bar F Ranch" is a St. Louis area Boy Scout reservation where I worked one summer.) If you understand them, great. If you don't, you haven't missed a thing, story-wise.

Where logical and legal I like to think everything I write happens in a single world. And the heroes and villains of others sometimes stick their heads in. Or receive a hat-tip.

The character Robert van Loan is related to, and possibly the father of, Richard Curtis van Loan. Dick van Loan is a World War One aviator who later becomes the Phantom Detective, the greatest sleuth of his generation. Franklin Havens' son, Frank, becomes a mentor of Independent Operators, including the Phantom Detective.

The Man From Blackhawk was an early 1960's TV western about an investigator for the Blackhawk Insurance Company. The only episode I now remember told how the hero journeyed to New York City to protect cartoonist Thomas Nast from the thugs of Boss Tweed and Tammany Hall. That show marked the first time I remember hearing about any of those involved.

And there are others.

Dime Novels, most actually costing five cents, were the self-contained fiction for the masses from before the Civil War until the beginning of the 20th Century. I enjoyed dropping them in throughout the narrative. The story of Buffalo Bill Cody's rides to Beadle & Adams' front door came from the book *Dime Novels*, a history of the publications released in the 1930s.

Watson mentions T.R.'s disgust about an Englishman's view of American flag ceremony. The book in question was actually published in the late twentieth century. And I was the one taken aback by the chap's point of view.

WARNING: Potential Spoilers below.

There really was a Deadwood Dick. And a bit of a wild man, from all accounts. The former slave is best known for riding his horse into a saloon and buying the animal a drink. Then his name got highjacked by the Dime Novel industry. So I combined the two.

And Mr. Stanley, the newspaper editor, was the lead character in the movie serial, "Deadwood Dick." One of the last few chapter plays, the budget was small. Stock footage abounded. And special effects were non-existent. Still the serial had its moments. And all three Deadwood Dicks appear in my story. Sort of.

I planned to chase the bad guys out of the ticker room with the smell of natural gas. From college chemistry I knew that the odor, in the form of a "mercaptan" is added before distribution. Good thing I checked into the history of natural gas. In the United States that chemical was not added until about 1930 after a school blew up killing about three hundred children and facility. Why would the industry wait that long? It boggles the mind.

ERWIN K. ROBERTS — has been a lot of things over the years. He started life as a charter U.S. Air Force brat. Now he is a retired Army/National Guard NCO.

At an early age he developed a fascination for adventure stories, fantasy, science fiction, comics, and heroic characters that continues to this day.

His varied jobs include radar operator, designing fast food parking lots, bureaucrat, audio/video technician, and Boy Scout camp staff. (But not necessarily in that order.)

In the 1980s and 1990s Erwin appeared about a thousand times on local cable TV programs in the Kansas City area. Often shooting, directing, editing and/or producing what he appeared in. For a brief time he hosted a nationally broadcast action movie show as Major A.D. Venture. (He never go paid for that, either.)

These days Erwin and his wife are empty nesters. They wait impatiently to become grandparents. (But the kids are not cooperating.) They recently celebrated their fortieth wedding anniversary by almost driving under a tornado. (Well, the Grand Canyon was sort of nice.)

These days Erwin writes for Airship 27, and others. (Too much writing, according to his wife.)

Erwin can be reached at erwin.k.roberts@gmail.com

Hound Dog Harker

In

"Hyde & Seek"

By Aaron Smith

Chapter One:
The Game is A Fist

Curtis Fleming did his best to avoid being noticed by the man he was following. Fleming was not inexperienced in the ways of stealth and subterfuge. His skills had been honed over many years of service to the British Intelligence Service. Now, at forty-nine, he was looking forward to his retirement. He hoped that his present assignment would be one of his last. Fleming had tailed the thin little man from his office, where he worked as an accountant, to a bar in the Whitechapel area of London where he had stopped for a pint after work. Now the target had left the bar and so had Fleming. The thin little man was walking briskly along the London streets in the rain, his umbrella open over his head. Fleming kept about thirty paces behind him, only his fedora keeping his gray-temple hair dry. The hat also served to keep the raindrops from obstructing Fleming's view by striking the lenses of his eyeglasses. The glasses were not needed, but Fleming wore them anyway; they helped to make him look like a harmless, shy, studious sort, the exact opposite of the clever spy that he had been for decades. He did not yet know why he was tailing this little man, only that his commanding officer, Colonel Sharpe, had given the order. It was not Fleming's way to question orders, only to see that they were followed to the letter.

Up ahead, the little man stopped. Fleming did the same, pretending to pick up a coin from the ground, in case the target should turn and look in his direction. Fleming glanced up and ahead from his bent over position. Thirty paces ahead, the little man lifted his nose and sniffed the damp night air. Fleming wondered what he was sniffing for. Had he noticed something? Had Fleming perhaps worn too much aftershave? Was that, a bit too much cologne, enough to give away the fact that someone was tailing the little man with the umbrella? Fleming waited, holding his breath.

The little man closed his umbrella…and he began to run. Fleming knew the following game was done. It had now become a chase. He yanked the glasses from his face and began to run after the target.

Down the rain-slick streets the two men ran, one pursuing the other. The little man tossed his umbrella aside and made a quick turn down a dark alley. Fleming skidded to a halt, his feet slipping as he hit a puddle. He struggled for a moment to keep his balance and then began to stride forward once more, intending to turn where his quarry had turned. As he walked towards the alley entrance, he thought he heard the sound of glass breaking, just a small, sharp shattering noise, like that of a bottle being dropped to the ground. He drew his gun, the standard, small, easily concealed pistol of men of his dangerous profession. Weapon at the ready, he turned into the alley. It was dark, shadows everywhere. He could hardly see, squinting as his eyes tried to penetrate the darkness. Then he saw it! Where was the short thin man? In front of Fleming stood the largest figure he had ever seen, a monstrous hulk of a man! Fleming's mind worked rapidly, sizing up the man who confronted him. The thing was huge; well over six feet tall, perhaps closer to seven, broad shouldered and immense. The darkness kept Fleming from seeing the giant's facial features, but he could see the ragged edges of torn clothing, as if the behemoth were literally bursting out of his clothes.

Fleming raised his gun, hoping the sight of it would frighten the large man into stillness. It didn't work. Faster than lightning, a huge fist swung forward! The gun fell to the wet ground as Fleming felt a terrible impact to the side of his skull. He felt nothing else. The lifeless body with the caved-in head fell to the rainy floor with a dull thud and a little splash. It was indeed his final assignment for the British Intelligence Service...but he would never get to enjoy his retirement.

The gigantic fist went back to rest at its possessor's side. The giant slowly lumbered down the alley and disappeared into the night.

Calvin "Picky" Pickover stood against the car, parked outside a small but well-kept house just outside London. The butler and chauffeur winced as a bloodcurdling scream came from inside the house. Pickover usually enjoyed working for his boss, Captain Quincy Harker of the British Intelligence Service, but sometimes, on occasions like this one, he hated it and longed for the life his father had lived, that of an ordinary butler, in the service of an ordinary English gentleman. Captain Harker was many things, but he certainly was not ordinary. Pickover began to hum an old song from his school days, trying to block out, from his mind if not from his ears, the terrible sound of newly discovered grief.

Inside the house, Elizabeth Fleming fell to her knees. She launched a long string of very unladylike profanities. Quincy Harker bowed his head, unsure of what else to say. After a full minute of cursing God, Mrs. Fleming drew in a deep breath, struggled to compose herself, stood up and

In front of Fleming stood the largest figure he had ever seen, a monstrous
hulk of a man!

offered Captain Harker a cup of tea.

An hour later, the new widow somewhat calmer, Harker walked outside. His cigarette was lit before he even got to the car. "Take me to the colonel's office, Picky," he muttered as the butler turned the key.

Harker did not speak at all during the drive into London. Curtis Fleming had been a colleague and a friend, and Harker would miss him. This, Harker thought, was why spies should never marry. This life was not one suited to men who wanted to settle down. Peaceful retirement was nothing more than a pipe dream. Men like Harker lived life fast and hard, savoring every moment, as they all knew—if they chose to be honest with themselves—that the next moment might turn out to be their last. Curtis Fleming had found that out the hard way, and now his widow had to live out the rest of her days without him.

By the time they reached their destination, Harker was done mourning. Now his mind turned to curiosity of the grim kind. He wanted to know how Fleming had died, and he wanted to know if there was anything he could do to avenge him.

Colonel Thurman Sharpe looked up from his paperwork as Harker entered his office. The old colonel did not look happy, but he rarely did. "Thank you, Captain Harker, for delivering that news to Fleming's wife. I'd have gone myself; I know it's an unpleasant task, but when one of my agents dies, there are certain matters that must take precedence."

"If I may ask, sir," Harker began, "How did Curt Fleming die? Was it part of an assignment, and can I take over where he left off? I'd hate to see it end there, whatever he might have been working on."

"Sit down, Harker," the colonel said. "Smoke if you'd like."

Harker took a seat and lit a cigarette, waiting for the colonel to begin his explanation.

"Fleming died from a blow to the skull," said Sharpe. "It was a powerful, crushing blow, smashing his brain in and probably killing him instantly. He didn't suffer much, if at all. Now normally we'd assume that such a blow must have been delivered by an object of some sort, so severe was the damage. However, our medical staff seems to think the impact impression matched that of a human fist...a very, very large human fist! So, we can conclude that Fleming's killer was a very big, very strong man, abnormally so. This assumption, Harker, raises an interesting problem. You see, Fleming was following a man when he was killed. But...the focus of his assignment was not a very large man; just the opposite. See for yourself."

Colonel Sharpe slid a photograph across the desk. Harker picked it up and looked. It was a picture of a small, thin man of forty or so. Judging by the background and the man's relation to it, he could not have been more than five feet, four inches tall. Harker judged him to weigh no more than one hundred and thirty pounds. There was no way such a diminutive man could have slammed his fist, even had it been an abnormally large hand, into Curtis Fleming's head with enough force to cave his skull in.

"This man couldn't have killed Curt," opined Harker. "But who was he? What was his name? Why was he being watched by our agency?"

"His name," Sharpe revealed, "was Cecil Masters. He was an accountant, aged forty-two. No criminal record. As you know, we have eyes and ears in all branches of the government, men who watch for any sign of aberrant phenomena of any sort that might signal a threat to our nation's security. Any indication of espionage, treason, or the like must be investigated. One of our men who monitors the post noticed that this man, a normal accountant and bookkeeper by all available accounts, had been receiving packages of the sort that tend to contain carefully secured liquids, usually chemicals of some sort. He alerted us and we did a careful check of all information available about Mr. Masters. He had no background in chemistry or any other science, save mathematics of course. Chemistry was not known to have been a hobby of his either. Why would such a man be receiving such packages? We thought it may have been nothing of consequence, but matters like this one must be investigated for the safety of all. So, I had Fleming follow the man for several days. Then we found him dead, in an alley, his skull smashed by what seems to have been an immense fist!"

Harker considered the information for a moment. He put out his cigarette in the colonel's desktop ashtray. "I'd like to volunteer to take over where Fleming left off, sir. But instead of simply following him, I'd like to hire him in a professional capacity, under an assumed name, of course. Perhaps it would be a better approach."

Colonel Sharpe nodded. "Go ahead, Harker. The case is yours. But do be careful. I don't want to bury two agents this week."

Chapter Two:
Madness in the Mountains

Albert Blakely tossed his stained lab coat aside and went out onto the balcony overlooking the snowy depths below his house and laboratory, hidden away in an isolated part of the Swiss Alps. He lit his pipe and smoked as he looked down into the drifting dunes of snow below. It was night and the black sky contrasted against the cold, white powder all around. Blakely smiled; satisfied at the work he had managed to do on that day. The formula was growing more potent with every new adjustment, every new test proving that he had made it better, and more powerful, longer lasting than the man who had first created it many decades ago.

Blakely was a wealthy man, to a certain degree. He had enough money to live quite comfortably, to have afforded this house in the mountains, to never want anything he could not afford...assuming he had the mind of most men. But his mind was different. Albert Blakely did not want a normal, calm life. He had no desire to fall in love, or marry, or have children, or live a life of hobbies and leisure. No; Albert Blakely wanted to rule the world, nothing more and nothing less. He had bought this house not to escape from civilization, but to work in...and pursue his plans without interruption.

Blakely was a genius when it came to science, and chemistry was his chosen specialty. He sought not the cures to disease or ways to grow better food or substances that could be used to improve industry. Rather, he sought the chemical means to conquer the world in which he had been born. He had built this house, and the laboratory that was hidden below the main floor, and the iron-walled cells that lay still further below the visible portion of the house, carved into the great mountains of Switzerland.

There, in his personal house of horrors, Albert Blakely toiled for hours, days, months, to decipher a carefully coded chemical formula that he had acquired at a secret auction held by one of the most powerful crime families in Italy. How the formula had come into the possession of the Scarvellis, Blakely did not know, nor did he care. He had had the money to win the auction, and he had the intellect to decipher the key to the code. He had used various connections to acquire the necessary components, and he had managed to duplicate the legendary formula. That had been the first step in his plan.

As a young student of chemistry, Blakely had read The Strange Case of

Dr. Jekyll and Mr. Hyde, a novella by the Scottish author, Robert Louis Stevenson, published in 1886. Blakely had immediately begun to wonder if the formula, the potion written about in the book, could be created in reality. He had researched the idea, and his curiosity had turned into sheer, power-hungry delight when he discovered that Stevenson had written, using fictionalized names and places, of true events! There had been a Jekyll, though that was not his real name, and he had indeed created a potion capable of unleashing a man's inner demons, and even of altering his physical body, evolving his form to match his attitude.

Blakely had searched long and hard to see if the formula for this incredible potion still existed. After years of grueling and sometimes expensive detective work, Blakely had learned that the formula did indeed exist, and it had somehow come to be among the property of the Scarvellis crime family. He had contacted them and learned that it would be among several strange items to be auctioned off. Blakely swore to acquire that formula, no matter the cost. Once he had the notebook in his hands, he spent months breaking the encryption and memorizing the formula. Finally, he burned the notebook—unwilling to risk ever having to share it with anyone—and set to work duplicating the amazing elixir.

Once he thought he had succeeded, he used his wealth to pay the Swiss government to release several criminals from prison. Taking advantage of these men's gratitude, he hired them to come and work at his mountain laboratory, where he intended to use them as test subjects in his quest to perfect his potion. Now, on this dark, snowy evening, he knew he was nearing success. He had come very close with his latest attempt, and had even sent some samples of the potion to his accountant in London, one Cecil Masters, for safe keeping. He had sent instructions for Masters to hide the small bottles where they could not be found, and to let them fall, under no circumstances, into the hands of the authorities. He awaited word that it had reached Masters, and he continued his experiments. Even now, there were three men locked in the cells beneath the house, all subject to the strange effects of the potion. Two had been successfully transformed, albeit temporarily, into huge, hulking monsters, capable of great strength, guided by great anger. The third man had shown some resistance to the elixir, and was now locked up, a drooling babbling specimen of insanity. *Oh, well,* thought Blakely, *that is the price of scientific progress. Sometimes a sacrifice had to be made.*

Blakely finished with his pipe and returned to the interior of his secluded home. As he retired to his bed for the night, he could hear the sounds of the three men in the cells below him; one a voice of grotesque savagery, growling and moaning like an animal in chains; the second, an incoherent babbling of insanities, like a religious fanatic squealing in tongues, a terrible Renfieldian noise from the bowels of Hell; and the third, a semi-normal human voice, crying out in English, albeit with a Swiss accent, "Bring me more! It is the nectar of God! I want to become myself again!"

Blakely smiled as he drifted off to sleep. Soon, he knew, he would rule over mankind. In this isolated house in the Alps, a king waited; a king and the beginnings of an army that would alter the course of human history for all time.

Chapter Three:
A Vial Experience

Quincy Harker was used to a certain style of clothing, a certain attitude, and a certain way of doing things. He liked to dress neatly but comfortably, liked to do what he wanted, when he wanted, and liked to appear as young and handsome as possible, mostly for the advantage of being able to attract as much attention as possible from the ladies. On this day, however, Harker was on the job, and that meant that his personal preferences had to be put aside in favor of what had to be done in the name of business. So, borrowing a page from Curt Fleming's book of tricks, Harker made himself look less like a dashing playboy and more like a business-minded investor. He left his usual slick-looking black suit in the closet and donned a tweed one instead. He put on a pair of unneeded eyeglasses like Fleming had often done, and he exchanged his usual cigarettes for a pipe. He picked up a briefcase full of faked financial papers and went on his way. His office had made an appointment for him; an appointment with a London accountant named Cecil Masters. For the purposes of the meeting, he would not be Captain Quincy Harker, but Lloyd Henderson, a successful businessman in need of some financial advice.

Harker soon found himself seated in Masters' office. It was a small office, not decorated, cluttered with papers and books, clearly the office of a man who was busy and cared little for appearances. Harker waited for ten minutes. The door finally opened and in walked Cecil Masters, a short, thin, timid looking man. Masters took off his hat and casually tossed it aside, aiming for an empty chair but not picking it up when he missed and it fell to the floor. He dropped his briefcase on the desk with a thump and sat down across from Harker. He did not smile or offer to shake Harker's hand. He immediately launched straight into the businesslike behavior that one might expect of a man who looked like Cecil Masters.

"What is it that I can help you with, Mr. Henderson?"

"Well, Mr. Masters," Harker, under his assumed name, began, "I fired my former accountant; stealing from right under my nose...or trying to at least, the dammed scoundrel! Now, Mr. Masters, my records have fallen into a heap of disarray and I need a man I can trust to straighten out this mess before I lose control of my business. I asked some colleagues for recommendations...

and your name came up, so here I sit, hoping you might accept me as your newest client."

"I see, I see," said Masters, scratching his whiskerless chin. "I shall need a few hours to go over your records before making a decision on whether or not I can fit you into my caseload. If you will be so kind as to come back in...."

Masters was unable to finish his sentence. His secretary, a grandmotherly looking woman, poked her head in the door and interrupted. "Mr. Masters, sir, could you come out here and sign some documents? I know you wanted them sent out immediately...but I need your signature."

Masters started to rise. "Yes, Mrs. Pennyworth. Excuse me, Mr. Henderson. I'll be back momentarily." He walked out of the room. Harker hoped the accountant would close the door behind him, and he did.

Harker was up in an instant. He had to act quickly, aided by his years of training and his own instincts and skills. He began to quickly, but methodically, search the contents of Masters' office. He made his way around to the other side of the desk, tossing his cigarette lighter under the desk so that he would have something to pretend to be looking for should his search be interrupted by the accountant's return. He opened the desk drawers, flipping through the stacks of papers contained therein. There was nothing of importance in the first drawer, and nothing in the second. He opened the third drawer, shoved aside some pens and papers and saw something worth finding. Several small vials of a red liquid sat in the corner of the drawer. Harker did not hesitate. He took one of the vials, shoved it into his jacket's inner pocket, retrieved his lighter from the floor, and darted back into his chair. He lit a cigarette, intending to use the act of apologizing for smoking in the office without permission as a distraction, should Masters suspect anything upon his return.

Masters came back in, sat down without a word on any matter other than business. "As I was saying, Mr. Henderson; if you would come back tomorrow at this time, I shall have had time to look through your documents and will be better prepared to accept or refuse you as a new client. You may trust that, whether or not we do further business, the contents of these files will be kept in the utmost confidentiality."

Harker agreed. He promised to return to Masters' office the next morning, and he got out of there as quickly as possible.

Harker called Colonel Sharpe's office to update his commanding officer on his progress, giving his impressions of meeting Cecil Masters and reporting his acquisition of the mysterious vial of liquid.

"Bring that vial in, Captain," said the colonel. "I'll have our department scientists take a look at it."

"If you don't mind, sir," replied Harker, "I think I know someone who can figure it out faster, and who is quite used to dealing with strange substances and strange events. Believe me, sir; he's completely trustworthy; I've known him my whole life."

"All right, Harker," Colonel Sharpe agreed, "but you'd better be right about this man, whoever he is. I'm holding you responsible if anything should happen to that liquid."

Harker ended his conversation with Sharpe and immediately went back to his large apartment in the heart of London to change back into himself. He discarded the tweed suit and got into his usual black one. He doffed the unnecessary spectacles. He put away the pipe and lit a cigarette. Businessman Lloyd Henderson was gone and in his place stood Captain Quincy "Hound Dog" Harker, hero of World War I battle fields, agent of the British Intelligence Service, relentless seeker of adventure and solver of mysteries. He called out to his butler and driver, Calvin Pickover, "Picky, fetch the car. We're going out again!"

Minutes later, Picky Pickover was driving towards the outskirts of London. Harker was in the backseat, reaching into his jacket pocket to be sure he had brought the small vial of red liquid with him. Not long afterward, the black car slowed to a stop in the driveway of a large, fairly expensive residence just outside the main city of London. Despite its proximity to England's greatest metropolis, this area was lovely, green and wooded, peaceful. It looked like a wonderful place to live.

Harker and Pickover got out of the car and walked up to the front steps. Harker rang the bell. Minutes later, the door swung open, revealing not a servant, but the lady of the house. She was a woman of early middle-age, still slim and petite, still as pretty as she must have been in her youth.

"Quincy! Picky! Hello, boys! I suppose you've come to see John, haven't you? That's how it always is now; never just stopping in for tea, always chasing some great mystery through the shadows…and popping up on our doorstep when chemical matters are involved! Well, you two are going to have tea anyway, whether you like it or not." After greeting them, she turned to the inside of the house and called for her husband. "John! Come out of that silly laboratory and come see who's here!"

Quincy Harker smiled a broad smile. He couldn't help it. He was at the home of old friends, people he had known and loved even in his earliest memories, and he always felt welcome in that house. He gave the woman a small kiss on the cheek.

"Clarice, you look lovely, as always," he said.

As Harker finished greeting the woman, the sound of footsteps and the sound of a cane came into the room. "Quincy...don't you go trying to steal my pretty young wife from me!" said the newest voice to come into the scene.

Harker turned around, smiling, to see a man in his late sixties, tall and slim, with a white beard and a lab coat standing there smiling back at him, holding up his cane in a jokingly menacing fashion.

"Hello, Doc!" said Harker, greeting his old friend, Dr. John Seward. Seward had been a friend of Harker's parents, Jonathan and Mina, since before young Quincy had been born. Seward and his wife, Clarice, had been frequent visitors to the Harkers' home during Quincy's childhood. Harker was also sure that Seward had played a role in what he called "The Incident," some event that had taken place in the lives of his parents before he was born, and of which the Harkers and friends never spoke. Even now, in his thirties, Quincy Harker still had no idea what the Incident had been, but he still had a great deal of curiosity about the matter. John Seward had been, for many years, the person in charge of one of London's most notable mental asylums. In recent years he had retired and now kept busy with his hobby of experimental chemistry. Since Harker's newest case now involved a mysterious red liquid, he had come to Seward to seek advice and scientific opinions.

"I take it this isn't a social call, Quincy. It rarely is, you being so busy with your government work," said John Seward. "Come, lad, let's go talk in the lab!"

Clarice Seward took Picky Pickover with her to the kitchen, saying something about making tea for her husband and Harker. Seward and Harker went down the hall to the room at the very end.

Seward's lab was a cluttered mess. The walls were covered from corner to corner with bookshelves; the center of the room had a large table with all sorts of beakers, burners, test tubes, containers of all shapes and sizes, and a ridiculously thorough assortment of other chemist's apparatus. The retired doctor obviously kept busy in his later years, and his never-waning enthusiasm always made Quincy Harker smile.

Seward sat down on a stool next to the large lab table. Harker stood beside him. He took the small vial of red liquid from his jacket pocket and held it up for Seward to see.

"I took this from a person of interest in a case I'm working on. You know I can't go into details, but I thought maybe you could help me figure out exactly what this is."

Seward took the vial from Harker. He pulled the stopper out of the top of the vial. He sniffed the contents, wrinkling his nose.

"Strong smelling stuff…quite acidic; I'm not sure what's in this stuff, but it's potent!" Seward judged. "I certainly wouldn't pour it into my brandy!"

"Can you do something, test it?" asked Harker.

Seward stood up and walked over to a small cabinet against the wall. The cabinet's door had several holes drilled in it; air holes, Harker assumed. He was proven correct when Seward opened the doors slightly, reached in, and produced a small white mouse. He brought the mouse over to the table and placed it inside a small wire cage. He picked up a tiny ceramic bowl, poured just a few small drops of the red liquid into the bowl, and put the bowl in the cage with the mouse. He closed the cage door.

"I hope this little creature is thirsty enough to try this stuff, despite the smell," said Seward. The two men watched.

The mouse did not hesitate. It put its head to the bowl and lapped up the red liquid as if it were milk. The bowl empty, the mouse stood still for several minutes. Harker and Seward kept a careful watch over their test subject.

Without warning, the mouse began to shake, to quiver and tremble violently. Seward and Harker watched with even greater attention. It looked as though the fur that covered the mouse was standing straight up on end. The muscles of the mouse's body began to throb and it looked to the two observers that the small rodent was actually beginning to grow larger! The mouse roared! It did not let out the small, timid squeak that one might expect to hear from such a creature, but literally growled! It was a harsh, predatory noise, greatly surprising both Harker and Seward. The mouse began to run wildly back and forth inside the cage, then running in circles, building up speed. It finally ran right into the bar of the cage, hitting hard, butting the wiry bars with its head! After the impact, it staggered backwards a few steps…and then fell over, slumped still on the cage floor.

"What the hell was that?" asked the shocked Quincy Harker.

Seward opened the cage door, put his hand into the cage and took the mouse out. He held the still, lifeless little creature in his hands and examined it.

"This mouse is dead," said Seward. "Look, Quincy, he fractured his skull when he ran into the cage bars! And we weren't imagining things either; this mouse is bigger than it was when I put it in the cage! Feel it; its muscles have grown and become more solid! Whatever that red chemical is, it increased the mouse's strength and sent it into a deadly frenzy!"

"Fascinating," was all Quincy Harker said.

Seward put the dead mouse down and picked up a pencil and a small writing tablet. He began scribbling some notes. "One can only imagine what might happen if a man were to ingest this substance!"

Chapter Four:
The Captain, the Kopp, and the Killers

arker checked in with Colonel Sharpe after leaving Dr. Seward's home. He informed Sharpe of the results of their experiment and the strange demise of the mouse. He took the vial, with the remaining portion of the red liquid, with him. Pickover drove him home and he decided to retire early for the evening and get the rest he might need for the next day. He intended to return to the office of Cecil Masters and interrogate the accountant. He saw no reason to keep up his guise as Lloyd Henderson when he could much better expedite the case as Hound Dog Harker. Harker, a man with much practice in putting his concerns aside and getting rest when he needed it, fell asleep with ease.

Harker was up early. He did not disguise himself this time, but dressed as he usually did. He decided to drive himself to Masters' office, rather than have Pickover take him there. He arrived near the office shortly after ten o'clock.

When he walked in, Masters' secretary informed him that Masters was already in and sent him through. Harker walked and gave a hearty "Good morning," to the accountant. He closed the door behind him. Masters looked up from a stack of papers and a startled expression crossed his face as he took note of Harker's change in appearance.

Harker didn't waste any time with conversation. He looked Masters straight in the eyes and demanded answers. "I'm here for some information, Masters. We're not talking about Henderson's finances anymore. There are other things we need to talk about!"

Masters began to stand up, but Harker drew his gun and aimed it at the accountant.

"Stay where you are, Masters, but keep your hands on top of the desk. Now, you're going to tell me where you got this....." Harker, still holding his gun in one hand, reached into his pocket with the other hand and took out the vial of red liquid. Cecil Masters' face went pale when he saw the vial.

"You...you have it!" Masters shouted, panicked. "That is mine! If he finds out you have it...he'll kill me...he'll send them to kill me!"

"Who?" demanded Harker, "Who will send who to kill you? Who sent you this liquid? If you don't tell me, he won't have to send them to kill you... because I'll put a bullet in your heart right here and now."

Masters looked at Harker and began to beg. "I'm assuming you are with the authorities, are you not?" Masters said. "You must protect me then! If I tell you his name and you do not take me and hide me somewhere...I will not live long! Please...I beg you...."

Harker found Masters' sniveling to be pathetic, but decided to use it to his advantage. "Fine; you'll have the protection of the government, if you tell me three things. I want to know who sent you this chemical substance, where I can find him, and who killed the man who was following you."

Masters began speaking again, his voice shaking with nervousness. "His name is Blakely; Albert Blakely. He is English...but I don't know where he is now. He sent me the liquid in unmarked boxes and I do not know his address. He may not even be in the country now. I will answer your third question because I do not wish for Blakely to have me killed...and I hope that you will not kill me now. I killed the man who followed me!"

"You!" exclaimed Harker, shocked that Masters was admitting to the murder of Curtis Fleming, even if he did fear for his life. He couldn't imagine how a small man like Fleming could have killed an experienced agent...and then it dawned on him. "You drank that liquid didn't you? You took that stuff and it made you crazy...and bigger!"

Masters nodded. "Yes. It is true. Take me away from here now. I am not safe."

Harker was disgusted by Masters and every bit of his behavior, but he resisted the impulse to kill him where he sat. He would not hesitate to kill when threatened, but Masters was unarmed. He picked up the telephone on Masters' desk and called for several men to come and take the accountant into custody.

Harker left as soon as the other agents arrived to take Masters out. He drove himself to headquarters and marched immediately up to the floor containing Colonel Sharpe's office.

"Have you ever heard the name Albert Blakely, sir?" Harker asked as he sat down in the chair opposite Colonel Sharpe's desk.

Sharpe shook his head. "I haven't, but I'd bet I will soon enough." He called his secretary into the room and had her immediately run down to the records division and see if there was a file on an Albert Blakely. Sharpe and Harker both smoked as they waited: Sharpe his pipe, and Harker a cigarette. The secretary, a fairly attractive brunette, walked into the office ten minutes later, deposited a thin file folder onto Sharpe's desk, and exited the room without a word. Thurman Sharpe, like a predator pouncing on his prey, grabbed the file and hungrily opened it, curiosity raging. He summarized out loud what he read.

"Albert Blakely, born in London, 1885, inherited a fair fortune upon his father's death; trained in biology and chemistry. It seems our boys have had an eye on him for some time; no hard evidence of any wrongdoing, but he aroused some suspicion when he sold his properties here in England and moved everything he has, lock, stock and barrel, to a house in the middle of a desolate part of the Swiss Alps, of all places!"

Harker had listened attentively to the colonel's synopsis of the file's content. "The Alps," Harker said when the colonel had finished. "At least now we know where those packages that were sent to Masters came from. But why would Blakely have this red serum? Did he create it and, if so, why? He must have sent samples of it to his accountant for safekeeping. I still have one sample and Masters, I think, ingested another one prior to killing Curt Fleming, but does Blakely have more of the stuff with him in Switzerland? And more importantly, what is he planning on doing with it?"

"That's what I want you to find out, of course, Captain Harker," said Colonel Sharpe, stating what was, to Harker, the obvious. "It could be nothing so dreadful after all. Perhaps he's going to sell this elixir of his to the Americans. That way their baseball players can hit more home runs!"

Harker laughed slightly, more at the idea that the stern-faced colonel had tried to make a joke than at the words themselves. "I suppose it's off to Switzerland for me then?"

Colonel Sharpe, now busy filling his pipe with new tobacco, just nodded. Harker left the room. Harker returned to his apartment to pack. He would travel light, taking only what he would need. He packed an extra suit, a warm coat, cigarettes, a few personal items, and extra ammunition for his gun. He would be travelling alone. Picky Pickover wanted to go with him, always the faithful butler, but Harker told him it would not be possible this time. Harker's other usual travelling companion, Billy Baxter—his friend who had been his sergeant when he had been an officer during the World War—was away on a family matter. Harker had been surprised to hear that, as he did not know that Baxter had any living family. He had almost asked for the details, but had decided against it. Every man is entitled to a few

"That's what I want you to find out, of course, Captain Harker."

little secrets, he reminded himself.

Harker, suitcase in hand, was dropped off at the airport by Pickover. He boarded a flight to Geneva.

The flight was a dull one. Harker had a drink and spent the time looking out the window, wondering what awaited him in Switzerland. There was not much else to do as the plane was not nearly full ,so he had a pair of seats to himself. On one hand he was glad, as one could never be sure what sort of person one might be seated with; on the other hand he was disappointed, as even the most inconsequential conversation can be a good way to pass the time.

The plane landed in Geneva and Harker disembarked. He lit a cigarette and sat on a bench, waiting for the Swiss policeman who was supposed to meet him there, someone called Inspector Kopp. Harker had no idea what the inspector looked like, so he hoped that Kopp had been provided with his description.

Ten minutes passed, then fifteen. Harker put out his cigarette and kept waiting. He was about to light another when he heard a voice behind him.

"Captain Harker; Captain Quincy Harker? I am Inspector Kopp," it said, and Harker stood up and turned around, startled at the type of voice it was.

"You're a girl!" Harker blurted out, unable to stop himself before he realized the rudeness of the statement. Inspector Kopp was, indeed, a woman...and a young one at that, much to Harker's surprise. She was about thirty, a long-legged blonde with a pretty face, perfect except for a thin scar that ran along her left cheek. Harker found the scar interesting; he decided that it added character to her appearance. Suddenly, Harker suspected that he might find himself enjoying this assignment more than he had anticipated.

"It's all right, Captain Harker. I'm used to the surprised looks," she said. "I am Analiese Kopp...and I assure you that I am just as capable of doing my job as any male officer. I am one of very few female police in Switzerland, but I am also among the best."

Harker liked her confidence and extended his hand just as he would towards a male colleague. He hoped that Inspector Kopp would perceive the gesture as a sign of respect.

The two agents, one British and one Swiss, found a bar and ordered drinks. They went right into discussion of the case, foregoing further pleasantries.

"The Swiss government is aware that Blakely has been paying our prison system to release certain criminals into his care," Analiese Kopp explained to Harker. "Of course, this aroused the suspicion of the government, but it was decided that we should allow it to happen, in the hopes that Blakely will implicate himself in whatever it is that he is doing out there in his little house in the mountains. As far as my superiors know, he is unaware that he is under any sort of investigation. He believes his success in having these prisoners released is due to the dishonesty of those he bribed for his purposes."

"And you have no idea," Harker asked her, "why he wants these prisoners sent to his home?" Inspector Kopp shook her head.

"Not yet," she answered, "but perhaps you can find out."

"And how will I do that?" was Harker's next question.

"By going to visit him," Kopp said, tantalizing Harker with the suggestion. "There will be danger involved though, I can assure you. It was brought to my attention earlier today that Blakely has made another payment to one of our prison officials. This time it was a larger payment, as he wants six prisoners sent to him, all hardened criminals, and murderers. Would you perhaps be interested in taking the place of one of these killers and using that ploy as a means to gain entrance to Blakely's house?"

Harker smiled. He liked the plan already; it wouldn't waste any time; it was direct and to the point. "It's an excellent idea, Inspector."

Chapter Five:
Nightmare in the Alps

The arrangements were made quickly. Inspector Kopp drove Harker to the nearest Geneva police station where the six prisoners had been brought to await transport to the house in the Alps. Harker was brought to a private room where he changed into clothing provided by the police department: trousers, a flannel shirt and wool jacket, with old, beat-up brown shoes. He had to look like a man with no money, a man just released from a long stretch in prison.

Harker saw Analiese Kopp for a moment more before he left. The Swiss policewoman looked Harker over. "You certainly look the part, Captain Harker," she said, fighting off the urge to laugh.

"You can call me Quincy, you know," said Harker, "or Hound Dog. That's what my friends call me."

"Quincy, perhaps," said the attractive inspector. "You don't look like a dog at all."

"I don't," said Harker, seeing no reason to fight off the urge to flirt with the woman before rushing off into a dangerous situation, "but I do chase what I want...until it can't run away from me any longer."

The two exchanged smiles and Harker turned and left. He was led, by two male police officers, into a small room where the five other prisoners were being held. He sat down with the others. They had been taken from several different prisons, so they did not all know each other, which would work to Harker's advantage. He glanced at the others. They ranged in age from, he guessed, twenty-five to fifty. They all had rough looks, hardened faces, and shifty, suspicious eyes. Harker maneuvered his own face into a wicked scowl; using his memory of criminals he had met in the past to fake a ruthless mean streak of his own.

The six men were herded into a transport truck, the doors were locked and then chained shut, and the truck, driven by one policeman with another riding shotgun, rolled onto the road. From what Harker had been told, they had only one road which led from the foot of the mountain to the area where Blakely's house was located. Once they reached that area, there was only one possible way in or out of their destination. Harker, unarmed and alone now, hoped his wits and experience would be enough to help him do what he had to do.

It was a long ride. Harker discovered that only one of the other prisoners spoke fluent English, a German who would only tell Harker his first name, Ernst. Of the others, two spoke mostly Italian, two French, and the last German, but not English. Although Harker could speak all of those languages to some extent, he saw no reason to reveal that yet and risk arousing suspicion that he might be more than a common criminal, so he conversed only with Ernst.

Ernst was in his mid-thirties, approximately the same age as Harker. He was a strongly built ox of a man, with huge hairy hands, which he bragged of using to strangle a romantic rival. He hinted that he had also killed several other men, but had not been caught for those other crimes. Ernst was a big, savage brute of a man, with a foul mouth and an obvious love of violence. Harker did not like him at all, but talking to an animal was better than passing the time in silence.

The back of the truck was windowless, so Harker had no view of the scenery. He could simply feel the winding, bumping roads going by beneath the truck. After what seemed like an eternity of rolling along, listening to Ernst's rude stories and the multilingual chatter of the other men, Harker could feel the truck begin to climb upwards, and he knew they had reached more mountainous terrain.

In his house atop the Alps, Albert Blakely knew that his latest shipment of men would be arriving soon. He had spent the day making preparations for their arrival. They were newly released prisoners, he knew, so he had to make certain precautions to keep them in line. For this, he would use the two men who had already been successfully made into his servants. Of the three prisoners he had previously kept in his home, he had personally shot one and dumped him in the snowy hills. That one had gone irrevocably insane in reaction to the red chemical serum and had to be put to death. The other two had reacted just as Blakely had hoped. When not under the influence of the drug, both had become quite loyal to Blakely. Why wouldn't they, when they depended on him for their next dose of the serum which made them better, stronger, more whole than they had ever felt before. Under the effects of the elixir, both were still loyal to Blakely, but their mental and physical characteristics were altered. One became stronger, more violent, a raging bull of a man. The other was sly, quick, and merciless. Both made excellent soldiers and dangerous killers. One of the conditions of service to Blakely's cause was that each man would give up his real name and be called by another name, a new name, a simple word that Blakely felt would best describe his unique talents, the talents that were brought to the surface when the elixir was consumed. The bigger of the two men would be known as Rhino; the smaller, faster one would be Jackal. Blakely would depend on Rhino and Jackal to help him control the new prisoners. He had no doubt that they were now his very willing servants.

Harker could feel the truck climbing higher and higher into the Alps. Finally, they came to a stop after the angle of the truck had evened out somewhat. The back door of the truck was torn open suddenly and the prisoners inside squinted as they saw daylight for the first time in many hours. The two armed policemen who had taken them on their journey stood in the chilly Alps air, aiming their rifles at the six men, gesturing for them to climb out of the vehicle.

The transfer of the prisoners from the police to Albert Blakely's men went quickly and without incident. The six men emerged from the truck and were held at gunpoint by the police until Rhino and Jackal appeared, training their own guns on Harker, Ernst and the others. The police officers climbed back into the truck and drove away, back down the narrow mountain road upon which they had come.

The six prisoners were escorted, still at gunpoint, to the large house that sat upon that lonely alpine peak. They were led inside, through large oaken wooden doors and found themselves in a cavernous room, devoid of furniture but warm and well-lit. The six men were told, by a mixture of words and hand signals, to line up with their backs to the wall. They did as they were told, and Rhino and Jackal stood there, still aiming those guns. The door to the rear of the room creaked open. Albert Blakely entered. Harker could tell that Blakely was a man of high intelligence and strong mental discipline. He could also detect a certain amount of wildness and perhaps even insanity in Blakely's eyes.

"Do any of you speak English?" was the first thing Blakely asked the new arrivals. Harker and Ernst responded in the affirmative.

"Good, good," said Blakely. Then the two of you shall be the first to learn why I have brought you all here. My two friends here, who I call the Rhino and the Jackal, will use their languages to explain things to the others. I ask that you two..." he gestured to Harker and Ernst, "will now follow me. I would advise you also to not entertain any ideas about violence or revolt. Remember that you are very high up in the mountains and it is quite cold outside. If you were to run from this place, you would surely freeze to death before you could reach the nearest village, even if you knew the way there. Remember also that I am your benefactor; I have freed you from prison and I can put you back there should you choose to defy me."

Blakely walked through the door. Harker and Ernst followed him. They walked down a long, barren corridor and stopped in front of another door. The door swung open, revealing another large room. It was windowless, lit by ceiling lamps. In the center were several chairs and a metal table. Along three of the room's walls were small jail cells; each containing a single bed and a toilet. They looked like the cells one might find in any police station, composed of iron bars in front, with solid walls on the sides and back.

"What is this?" muttered Ernst, in English, in his thick German accent, "Another prison to replace the old one?"

Blakely interrupted Ernst's complaining query. "No, my friend, not a prison, but a place of science and progress; the abode of miracles and the birthplace of a new world empire…an empire of which you will be a great soldier!"

Harker spoke next, risking an interruption to Blakely's speech to keep Ernst from having another strong outburst. Harker thought his best bet was to keep Blakely calm until he could determine precisely what was going on in this strange house in the Alps.

"An empire," Harker asked, "What exactly do you mean by that? I'm interested to know more. It seems you didn't buy my way out of that rotten prison for nothing!"

Blakely smiled. From Harker's manner of speaking he guessed that he was encountering a man of some intelligence, the type of man that perhaps he could come to respect.

"I know by your accent that you are a fellow Englishman," Blakely said to Harker. "Welcome to my home. I think you will find what I have to say to be very, very interesting indeed."

Blakely took out a cigarette case from his pocket. He noticed Harker's hungry look and opened the case, holding it out to the undercover British agent. Harker happily accepted a cigarette. Blakely lit his own cigarette and then held his lighter for Harker to use the flame for his. The first inhalation of the hot smoke was wonderful for Harker, who had not smoked since just prior to assuming the guise of a convict. Ernst stood to the side of the two Englishmen, grumbling to himself as if insulted by being left out of the conversation; he had not been offered a cigarette.

"What is your name?" asked Blakely of Harker, "And why were you incarcerated?"

"The name is Arthur Quincy," said Harker, not quite lying, since Arthur and Quincy were, indeed, two of his several given names, with Quincy being the one he had answered to most often since his childhood. "I was in jail for killing a man, though I'd like to make it clear that I never did confess to such an act…and I won't now, either."

"It matters little to me if you did it or not," said Albert Blakely, "only that you are capable of such an action if given sufficient reason." As he spoke, he walked over to the metal table in the center of the room. He reached under the tabletop and grabbed hold of a handle; he pulled. Harker watched as a slim, shallow drawer slid out from under the table. Blakely's hand reached into the drawer and then emerged again. When it came out, it was holding a strange sort of pistol; a silver gun with a black handle, of a model that Harker, despite being trained in the recognition of different sorts of firearms, had never seen before.

Before Harker could ask about the odd-looking weapon, Blakely whirled about in one swift motion, raised the gun at Ernst's chest, and pulled the trigger! The brawny German's face registered shock and alarm as he instinctively tried to move out of a bullet's path, but he was not fast enough. Much to Harker's surprise, there was no loud *'bang!'* but only a sharp whistling sound, followed by the soft *'thhpt'* of something embedding itself in Ernst's chest, just under the left shoulder. The big German's eyes rolled back in his head and then closed. The strong solid body fell backwards and hit the bare floor with a crash. Ernst was unconscious, but Harker could tell by the rising and falling of his chest that he was alive.

Blakely stared down at Ernst for a few minutes, and then looked back at Harker. "I thought perhaps I would give a demonstration rather than a long winded speech about my work here. This, I think, is a quicker way to satisfy your curiosity, Mr. Quincy."

Blakely bent down over Ernst's fallen body and lifted it by the shoulders. Blakely was not a large man and he began to drag the body before glaring up at Harker. "Don't stand there, Quincy. Assist me!"

Harker lifted Ernst's feet and the two men carried the unconscious German into one of the little cells. They tossed him onto the bed, which looked ridiculously small and bent slightly under Ernst's two-hundred and sixty pound frame. Harker stepped back and kept watch on Blakely's next actions. Blakely reached, once again, into his pocket and took out something which Harker recognized immediately: a small vial of red liquid!

Blakely yanked the stopper out of the top of the little vial. He bent over

Ernst and pried the German giant's jaws open. He poured the vial's contents into Ernst's mouth and then squeezed Ernst's throat. Harker saw that the touch on the throat was some sort of technique to cause an involuntary act of swallowing. The red serum consumed by Ernst, albeit while asleep, Blakely walked out of the cell and motioned for Harker to follow. When both men were outside the barred chamber, Blakely slammed the door and tugged on it to assure himself that it was securely locked.

"Now, Mr. Quincy, we shall sit and smoke some more as we await the results of what I just did to your large friend."

Harker and Blakely had sat for nearly an hour on two chairs that stood beside the table in the otherwise empty center of the cell-lined room. Each had smoked three cigarettes, Blakely having generously shared his tobacco supply with his fellow Englishman. Harker thought it was a shame that Blakely was the subject of an investigation. Had circumstances been different, Harker thought that he and the eccentric chemist could have been friends. Blakely actually reminded Harker of a younger and perhaps darker reflection of his dear friend, John Seward.

As both men simultaneously snuffed out their third cigarette, the sound of a low-pitched groan came from Ernst's cell. Harker and Blakely shifted their attention from their idle conversation to watching the small, barred room that held the captive German brute.

Ernst opened his eyes. He groaned again. Then he moved, swiftly, suddenly, startlingly fast for a man of his size, and he was on his feet! He let out a ferocious growl, the sound reverberating throughout the cavernous room. His eyes shone with animalistic fury as Harker had rarely seen in human beings.

"Let me out!" bellowed Ernst in German. "I must be free! I will kill you!"

He threw himself at the bars of the cell. Harker, amazed, could see the strong iron bars actually move a bit; Ernst, in maniacal fury, had managed to move them!

Albert Blakely smiled. "Do you see, Mr. Quincy, the incredible power of the potion which I forced down the throat of your large friend? Such is the effectiveness of this serum that it had brought to the surface all the rage, all the power, all the terrible potential strength that this man possesses; all his utter hatred and fury!"

Harker nodded. "I see that. Most impressive," he said, trying to sound fascinated, but internally horrified at what Blakely's elixir had unleashed.

Ernst looked every bit as unhinged and reasonless as the mouse in Seward's lab had looked before bashing itself to death against the bars of its much smaller cage.

"Next," Blakely continued, "I shall entice this man, much as Pavlov did with his dogs, to obey me. Like the others you saw, the men I call Rhino and Jackal, this man shall be one of many soldiers who will obey me and use this unlocked potential for destruction to bring the world to its knees... and lay it at my feet. This discovery, this great miracle of science, shall make me a king among men!"

Harker thought for a moment before asking the obvious question. He knew it had to be asked and he feared that he could anticipate the answer already.

"I suppose you expect me to drink that stuff, too."

Blakely smiled. "I certainly do, Mr. Quincy. I think you will find it to be a most enlightening and illuminating experience. I predict, if I may, that the results of your ingestion of the serum shall prove to be much different than the results we are seeing in this heavily built German. You, Mr. Quincy, unless I greatly misjudge you, are a man not only of strong will, but one of intellect as well. Perhaps those qualities will be magnified by the serum. Should my guesses prove correct, you may, I think, make an excellent second-in-command for my army of supermen, answering only to me!"

Harker thought about what to say next. Since Blakely seemed to like him, he decided he could get away with asking one more question without arousing suspicion.

"Aren't you worried that word of your plan might leak out of here somehow? What if the police or the military should learn of your experiments? What's to stop them from storming this place in large numbers? This house is secluded, but it's not a fortress by any means."

Blakely shrugged and laughed. "Mr. Quincy, in either event—the success of my plans—or their failure, I have taken steps to ensure that my name will grace the history books. You see, there are several small towns and villages far below this mountain peak. I have concealed a great quantity of explosives beneath this house. Should my mountain manor ever come under attack, the simple flipping of a switch shall detonate those explosives...and send a massive avalanche down on those little people far below! With one simple sweep of my hand, thousands will die! I shall either rule this world...or leave it with great infamy!"

Harker mentally sighed in relief; he thought about how fortunate it was that he had decided to sneak into Blakely's presence in disguise rather than simply lead a charge of Swiss police.

"Now, Mr. Quincy," said Blakely, "it grows late. Tomorrow you shall have your first taste of my wonderful serum. For tonight, you should rest. You have had a long journey and, I hope, an interesting experience. Outside this room, you will find my assistant, Jackal. He will escort you to your quarters. I will remain here and tend to our German friend. Good night, Mr. Quincy."

Harker turned to leave the room and then changed his mind. He paused. "Do you think I could have a few cigarettes for the night?"

"Certainly, my friend!" said Blakely. He reached into his pocket and pulled out a packet of cigarettes, a full one, which he had on his person in addition to the one from which the previously smoked cigarettes had been taken. "With my compliments...and here is a book of matches, too."

Harker left the room and met Jackal in the hallway. The wiry, merciless looking man held his gun on Harker and took him down the hall to a small bedroom. Harker went inside; in the room was a single bed, a sink, a toilet, and an empty glass atop the sink. There was no window. It wasn't much better than Ernst's cell, Harker told himself, but at least it had some privacy. Behind Harker, Jackal slammed the door. Harker knew by the sound it made that it had locked upon closure. He would not be leaving that room until Blakely decided to let him out. He opened the pack of cigarettes, took one out and lit it, and sat on his bed, wondering what had become of the other four men with whom he'd arrived.

Harker awoke to the sound of his door opening. He had slept peacefully, despite being where he was. Now, he saw that it was Rhino, the larger of Blakely's two soldiers, who had come to wake him. Rhino carried no weapon this time, but carried himself with brute confidence that would make any intelligent man think twice before trying anything with him. He motioned for Harker to get up, then turned and walked out into the hallway. Harker, who had slept in his clothes, stood and followed.

Blakely had gathered everyone in a large dining area: Harker, Rhino, Jackal, the four other prisoners, and even Ernst, who looked much like he had before being made to swallow the serum, but did not speak and had a dull, glazed expression in his eyes. Blakely sat at the head of the table and did most of the talking as the others ate. The breakfast was splendid—coffee, ham and eggs, excellent freshly baked bread, bacon— Harker wondered where the warm soft bread had come from; Rhino and

Jackal certainly didn't look like bakers. Had Blakely baked it? An insane megalomaniac chemist who also cooked? That was something Harker had never considered before.

Despite talking throughout breakfast, Albert Blakely actually said very little. He went on and on about how wonderful it was to have everyone there and how they were all privileged to be a part of such historic events. Rhino and Jackal translated. Once Harker realized that Blakely's speech was going to be quite repetitive, he tuned it out and concentrated on his breakfast.

When the morning meal had ended, Blakely instructed Jackal and Rhino to lead the five prisoners, excluding Harker, to the main laboratory area. There, Harker assumed, the five men would be drugged and locked into cells as Ernst had been on the previous night. Judging by the dazed expression on Ernst's face, he wouldn't put up much resistance against being locked up and experimented upon again.

Once the others had departed down the hallway, Harker stood alone with Blakely.

"Come with me, Mr. Quincy," said Blakely. "My assistants are more than capable of tending to your fellow guests. I have a special interest in you, as I said last night. Join me in my study, if you would."

Not that I have a choice, thought Harker as he followed Blakely into a small room. Blakely's study was a fairly typical office with a desk, several chairs, and bookshelves that ran from floor to ceiling on two walls. A quick glance at the books' spines showed Harker that the shelves contained a mixture of scientific texts and the classics of literature. He noticed Shakespeare, Chaucer, Dante, Doyle, Dickens, Stevenson (from whom Harker correctly guessed that Blakely had gotten the idea for his serum), and many other authors of note. The room also had a window, a large pane of glass without curtains. It was, Harker mentally noted, the first window he had seen since he had entered Blakely's alpine abode the day before.

Blakely sat down behind his desk. Harker sat across from him. They both lit cigarettes. Harker noticed that Blakely was staring at him, as if mentally weighing his thoughts and opinions of Harker. After several minutes of silence, Blakely spoke.

"Mr. Quincy, I believe it is time for you to test, for yourself, the fruit of my labors here in this house. I judge you, as I said last night, to be a man of intelligence and great potential." He opened his desk drawer as he spoke, and took out a vial of the red serum. "I offer you a taste of this, the bringer of strength, the magnifier of great qualities. Drink it and become what you were always meant to be!"

Harker had been dreading the moment when Blakely would propose such a thing. He had sworn to himself that he would never consume Blakely's strange red elixir. Now he had to act; he had no choice.

Harker stood and moved towards Blakely's desk as if to take the serum from the chemist's hand. He reached out, took the vial from Blakely. He pulled the stopper from the vial's top…and threw the liquid in Blakely's face!

Blakely howled as the serum hit him in the eyes. He reached up and wiped it from his face, spitting out the few drops that had gone into his mouth.

"Traitorous scum!" he screamed at Harker. "I trusted you, Quincy! You could have achieved immortality at my side!"

Harker had to get out of there. He knew the fury in Blakely's words and expression. He had seen similar insane rage in the criminal kind before. He knew he would not be allowed to live for very long should he remain in Blakely's presence.

"Jackal, Rhino…come to me! We have been betrayed!" Blakely shouted.

Harker put his hands over his face to protect his eyes and threw himself at the office window. The glass shattered as Harker dove through. He landed outside, rolling in the snow. He stood and brushed the snow from his pants and shirt and then began to run. He darted into the forested area that ran along the mountaintop behind Blakely's house. Behind him, he could still hear the mad chemist shouting, barking for his lieutenants to come to his aid. He glanced back once and saw the huge body of Rhino squeezing himself through the broken window. He was armed with a pistol.

Harker was alone, unarmed, and dressed in clothes very unfit for the winter weather of the Swiss Alps. He could not, however, reverse his course now. He kept running, hoping he could at least outrun the large, lumbering Rhino. He was glad to see that, so far as he could tell, the smaller and swifter Jackal had not yet joined the chase.

Harker felt the cold air of the Alps bite into his face, but he ignored it. He was concerned with survival against the Rhino, who was surely intent on killing him. He would worry about staying warm later. He could hear the snow crunching underfoot as the huge man chased him across the mountaintop. There were trees all around and Harker had to dart between them as he ran. He could feel that the land was beginning to decline. He was going downhill; the ground beneath his feet growing steeper. He knew that he could use this sloping of the geography to his advantage. He was a man of average, though muscular, build, thus he was fast and agile. He could maneuver quickly on steep ground and move easily between trees. He knew that a larger man, like Rhino, would be slower, not as quick to maneuver. That, Harker decided, might be the difference that determined whether he survived.

A loud *'crack!'* split the alpine air behind Harker. *Dammit,* he thought, *he's shooting at me!* Harker did not think Rhino was close enough to see him yet, from his position behind and above, so he assumed that Rhino was just taking shots, aiming randomly and hoping for luck. Harker wished he had a gun himself, but he kept moving, trying to keep as far ahead of the charging Rhino as possible. Another shot rang out, then another; Harker knew that even without a visual target, Rhino just might manage to send one of those bullets in the right direction at the right moment.

Harker decided to change his strategy. Continuing to run would wear him out and he suspected that Rhino's endurance might be improved by Blakely's serum. *Better to stop and fight him*, Harker thought, *than let him catch me exhausted!*

Harker stopped. He jumped up and grabbed a long, fairly thick, low hanging branch from a tree. The weight of Harker's body snapped the dry wood and the branch broke off. It was just what Harker had wanted. Broken branch in hand, he ran just a bit further. Then he stopped again as he saw a tree with a thicker trunk and some thick brush on the ground beside it. He crouched down behind the tree, behind the brush, hoping he was thoroughly concealed. He waited.

The crunching of Rhino's heavy steps upon the snow-covered ground grew louder as the brute drew near. Finally, he was right on top of Harker's position. Rhino was about to run past. The branch jutted out from behind the tree, prompted by Harker's hand. Rhino tripped! The gun flew from his hand and slid down the steep mountainside. The now unarmed giant was face down in the snow.

Harker did not waste any time. He stood and came up behind Rhino as the hunter struggled to stand. Harker swung that branch like a battle axe and brought it crashing down on Rhino's back! The branch broke, stunning Rhino only momentarily. He reached back with an arm and a huge fist and swatted Harker like an insect!

Harker now fell on his back. The fall knocked the wind out of him, but his toughness allowed him to keep his wits about him; he looked up to see Rhino standing over him with raging bloodlust in his eyes. Harker had not, even when he fell, let go of the half of the branch that he held after it had snapped in two. Gritting his teeth in distaste at what he had to do, he pushed upward with the makeshift spear...impaling Rhino in the abdomen! The big pursuer's face twisted, first in shock, then in agony. He groaned once and fell forward, landing atop Harker and pinning him to the snowy ground.

Harker moaned as the impact of the big man came down upon him, but he felt no bones break, no injuries, only the weight. He gave a heave and pushed the corpse off of him and to the side. Then he rose and brushed the now crimson snow from his clothing. He shivered once, his teeth chattering against each other...and he fled from the gruesome scene, continuing carefully down the mountainside.

Trying to keep the cold from his mind, he kept walking, moving along as fast as he could, stumbling occasionally as the wooded, snow-covered ground grew steeper and steeper. On and on he walked as the day wore on. He grew hungry, he got tired, and his eyelids grew heavy. Dusk came and went and he continued on, struggling to see in the darkness of night. He kept reminding himself to flex his fingers to avoid frostbite. He shoved his hands into his pockets. Slowly, but steadily, he began to forget where he was, where he was going. Like an automaton, only his muscles retained will, only his body kept going forward; his mind went blank with exhaustion. Finally, after many hours of struggling on, Harker collapsed to the ground and tumbled into the blackness of sleep.

Chapter Six:
Now You See Him...

Harker's head ached. That was the first sensation he felt; a sharp, throbbing pain that thumped through his brain, again and again like the impact of a jungle drum being pounded by a native over and over. The pain was the first sign of consciousness to greet him. He hesitated to open his eyes, fearing that the light would increase the agony of the headache. He waited for only seconds, but those seconds felt like hours. His eyelids parted and the overhead lamp shone down in his face. He let out one long, miserable groan and then forced himself to sit up. The room spun around him as he sat, but his wits were present enough for him to evaluate his surroundings. He was in bed, covered to his chest with a white blanket. His sense of touch told him that, despite some pain throughout his frame, he was bodily intact. He breathed a sigh of relief. The headache began to lessen. His most vivid feeling at that moment was one of complete and utter exhaustion. He felt mentally foggy and struggled to remember how he had arrived in this bed, in what he assumed was a hospital somewhere. He knew it would be futile to attempt to get up, since he nearly lacked even the stamina to sit, never mind stand. So, Harker sat and waited, feeling his strength and presence of mind return, though very slowly.

After some time, he heard a knob turn and the door opened. Harker's spirits immediately lifted as he saw the tall, blonde Inspector Analiese Kopp walk into the room. The sight of a woman, especially one so attractive as Kopp, could remedy almost any ill that Harker suffered.

"Good afternoon, Captain Harker," said Inspector Kopp. She smiled and Harker smiled back as best as he could.

"Afternoon..." Harker mumbled. "Afternoon of what day?"

"It is Sunday," Kopp replied in her deep Swiss accent, which Harker had decided added to her appeal.

"Sunday!" Harker nearly shouted; shocked to realize how much time was just a blank space in his memory. "But it was Thursday. What happened? How did I get here...wherever this is?"

Inspector Kopp, disregarding the etiquette that would normally be present between a man and a woman who hardly knew each other, came closer and sat down on the edge of the bed. "How do you feel?" she asked.

"Sore, tired, hungry, and confused," was Harker's answer. "But I need an explanation. What happened?"

Inspector Kopp began to explain. "I'm sure you recall being sent up the mountain to Blakely's house with that truckload of prisoners. I hope you can remember what happened up there, because it's vital to our case. I can tell you what happened after that. You were found on Saturday morning, very early, even before sunrise. One of the local villagers, an old man, came across you, unconscious on the ground, several miles from Blakely's house. You were cold, perhaps even close to death. Your clothes were torn and tattered and stained with blood, although the blood does not seem to have been yours. The old man tried to wake you up, but he could not…so he dragged you to his home, covered you with blankets by the hearth, and then walked five miles to the nearest telephone. He called the police. That old man saved your life. You'd not have lasted another hour out there in the snow."

"I'll be sure to go and thank him when I get out of here," Harker said. "I'm trying to recall how I got there to begin with. Bear with me, Inspector; it will all come back to me. I'm sure of it."

The Swiss policewoman smiled. "You told me to call you Quincy, or Hound Dog…but I'll stay away from the more canine of those names. Please…we're not out in the field right now, so I'm Analiese. All right, Quincy?"

"That works for me," said Harker. He smiled back at her, wondering if what had just crossed his mind had crossed hers as well. Then he drifted back into the land of dreams.

Several hours later, Harker was awake again and strong enough to sit up and eat. A nurse brought him a plate of food: sausage, potatoes, eggs, and coffee. He greedily gulped it down, not looking up from his plate even for a moment. He had no desire to look up, since the nurse, a thickly built Swiss woman with a ruthless scowl to her face, reminded him strongly of a particularly obnoxious major he had once served under when he had been in the regular British Army.

He finished eating and Helga (which was probably not her name, but Quincy had begun to think of her as such) took the plate away with not a single spare crumb left behind. Harker sat back in bed and wished for a cigarette.

As if in answer to an unspoken prayer, the room's door swung open again, this time revealing not one, but three visitors. Harker, delighted, sat

"How do you feel?" she asked.

straight up and grinned.

"Now don't tell me you all flew out here to Switzerland to see me!"

Colonel Thurman Sharpe, Doctor John Seward, and Harker's butler, Picky Pickover stood there looking at Harker. Seward and Pickover were smiling. Sharpe had on his usual mask of sternness.

"I came here, Captain Harker, to see to the successful completion of this mission, not for pleasantries," snapped the colonel.

"Well, I'm certainly happy to see you, lad," said Seward, "and so is Picky here."

The butler stepped forward and tossed a packet of cigarettes to Harker. Despite his tiredness, Harker caught it, tore the wrapper open, took a cigarette out and waited as Pickover produced a lighter. Harker inhaled deeply and realized that he was finally beginning to feel like himself again.

"Captain Harker," said Colonel Sharpe, "You seem to be fine, so I want a full report immediately!"

For the next thirty minutes, Harker told his visitors about everything; his arrival at Blakely's house, the way Blakely had taken him under his wing, the incredible results of giving the red serum to Ernst, his escape through the window, the fight with Rhino and, most importantly, the explosives buried under the house, which were the primary reason that great caution had to be taken when it was decided what to do next in regards to the problem of Blakely's insane plan for world domination through the creation of an army of elixir-enhanced warriors. The colonel listened with great attention, as if filling the filing cabinet of his brain with all relevant facts. He nodded quite often. Seward listened but did not speak. He seemed to be pondering each detail as Harker related it. Pickover, never the most stout-hearted of men, let out an occasional whimper of "Oh, my," each time Harker got to one of the more grisly parts.

A day later, Harker was well enough to get up, get dressed, and leave the hospital. Pickover and Seward had gone sightseeing in Geneva. Colonel Sharpe had met up with his counterpart in the Swiss security service and had gone to lunch. Harker walked out of the hospital and lit a cigarette. He glanced around the street he had walked out onto and wondered what to do while he waited for the others to return. Happily, he saw Analiese Kopp walking up to him. The two were soon in the bar where they had had their first drinks together only a few days before. They used up a few hours there, talking, drinking, getting along well, before returning to the local branch of Kopp's agency to meet both her superiors and Colonel Sharpe. Doctor

Seward had also joined them, though not Picky Pickover, whom Colonel Sharpe would not allow to be present at official briefings.

"It seems we have a bit of a problem here," said the colonel. "We now know what this Albert Blakely person is planning on doing. As strange as it all sounds, if that's what Harker says he found out, then that's the story. Now we need to figure out what to do about it. The problem is that Blakely claims he's got enough explosives up there to bring the whole damned mountain, and all that snow, down on the heads of those civilians that live below it. He might be bluffing...but he might not, and we can't afford to take that risk. If that weren't the case, I'd say we should just attack the place with every man we've got...but we can't do that, can we? If any of you have better ideas, speak your minds."

Harker was silent, Kopp was silent, and the other Swiss police were silent. Sharpe looked around disappointedly. Finally, the silence was broken by the sound of Seward clearing his throat. "Colonel, gentlemen, Miss Kopp, umm...I mean Inspector...I know I'm not a member of any of your agencies, but I think I might be able to help!"

Harker spoke before anyone else could. "Seward, I knew you'd have an idea! What is it?"

"Well, first," said the bearded old doctor, "I'm going to require certain chemical components...in rather large quantities."

Six hours later, as Seward had asked, Sharpe, Harker, and Kopp joined him in one of the laboratories usually used by the Swiss medical examiners. They walked in to find Seward in a lab coat with a large assortment of bottles on the table, and a bathtub on the floor, filled with a sky blue liquid. There were three stools next to the table and Seward asked the others to sit down as he explained what he had been doing for all those hours.

"When Captain Harker came to my home and showed me the serum developed by this Blakely fellow, and I saw the effects it had on that poor laboratory mouse, I was immediately reminded of a certain old story, that of Dr. Jekyll and Mr. Hyde.

"Once my mind had entered a cycle of thinking of lurid stories, it turned to the subject of another author, H.G. Wells. His book, The Invisible Man, featured a character who used a scientific method to alter the way his body reacted to light, thus rendering him invisible! It occurred to me that if this Blakely had managed to duplicate what Stevenson had written about in his story then perhaps it would also be possible to do what Wells had suggested. I liked the idea for about five minutes...until I decided that it was no more than the idle fantasy of a silly old man! I went back to more serious thoughts. But...as I slept that night, the idea returned to me and I lay in bed, half-awake, thinking about it. So strongly did the idea implant itself in my brain, that I had to try.

"I concocted several mixtures of chemicals, giving each one to my test mice. The thirteenth mouse...actually vanished from my sight! At first I thought I had simply neglected to close his cage properly and he had escaped, but I stuck my hand in and the little devil scratched me! I was dumbfounded! I had actually succeeded! The potion wore off after three hours and the little creature came back within the range of my sight. Unfortunately, there was a slight flaw in the chemical mixture, for when the poor mouse was visible again, he was also dead!"

Colonel Sharpe, Captain Harker, and Inspector Kopp just stared at Seward. They were all amazed by what the old doctor had just told them. Harker was the first to react verbally.

"Ha! You outdid yourself this time, Doc! But I don't see how it helps us if it killed the mouse."

Seward laughed. "I didn't think it would have any use either, Quincy. Then I had an idea. That's why I've made such a large amount of the stuff here in Geneva. That's what this bathtub is filled with." He pointed at the blue-liquid filled tub on the floor by the table. "Inspector Kopp, would you be so kind as to lend me one of your gloves?"

Analiese Kopp nodded and slipped the brown leather glove from her left hand and gave it to Seward. Seward put the glove on the table and then picked it up again with a pair of metal tongs. He used the tongs to dip the glove into the tub of chemicals. When he pulled the tongs out of the tub, they appeared to be empty. Seward opened the tongs and the three observers heard the wet slap of the glove—though they could not see it— hitting the floor!

"You see, my friends, how it works! Inspector Kopp, would you pick up the glove and put it back on, please? Don't be afraid; the chemical mixture cannot hurt you unless you drink it."

Kopp did as she had been asked. Harker watched, expecting the glove to be simply transparent so that Kopp's hand would appear to be bare even when covered by the glove, but to his surprise, the glove and the hand it contained were now invisible! It looked as if the inspector's arm ended at her wrist, the floor visible beneath the place where everyone knew her hand really was! The area was slightly blurred, but in a way so inconspicuous that one would only notice it if one knew to look for such a visual distortion. Even Colonel Sharpe was impressed. "Magnificent!" exclaimed the supervisor of spies.

"So you see," continued Seward, "when an object is rendered invisible, the object contained within it, the inspector's hand in this case, is also removed from the range of our vision. It occurred to me that this could be an excellent solution to the problems often faced by those in the same profession as my dear friend, Captain Harker!"

"Absolutely," agreed Harker. "All we need to do is dip all my clothes in this mystery juice of yours…and I can sneak right back into Blakely's house and end his mad scheme once and for all! I'll need a suit that covers everything from head to foot, and we'll need some sort of goggles too, so my eyes can't be seen. A pair of floating eyeballs would attract too much attention."

Sharpe nodded. "All right, Harker. I'll get you that suit."

"Make those two suits, Colonel," interjected Analiese Kopp. "I'm going with him." She took the invisible glove off and looked down at her hand, flexing her fingers as if she were glad to see them again. "This is going to be fun."

Chapter Seven:
Blood in the Snow

A plan was quickly formulated, one that earned the approval of both Colonel Sharpe and the head of the equivalent Swiss agency. It was decided that Harker and Kopp would go in alone, infiltrating Blakely's home under the cover of invisibility. They would, at the very least, disarm the explosives that Blakely supposedly had ready under the house. Once this was accomplished, they would signal for help by shooting flairs into the sky. When the flairs were seen, a large squad of Swiss police would storm the mountaintop house. Both Harker and Kopp were under orders not to engage in violent confrontations with Blakely or his underlings unless it was impossible to avoid. The first objective was to render the explosives harmless. After that, Blakely would be dealt with. When all had agreed on the proper course of action, the plan was put into motion.

A truck, painted to look like an old, dilapidated vehicle used by local residents, was sent up the mountain road. Harker and company hoped that if Blakely or anyone else saw the truck from up on the mountain, they would assume it was just the locals going about their business. Inside the truck were Harker, Kopp, and a Swiss police lieutenant who would do the driving. The small truck made its way three quarters of the way up the ever-steepening mountain road. It stopped there and the driver called into the back of the truck to alert Harker and Kopp that it was time to begin the next phase of the operation.

Harker and Kopp, putting modesty aside in favor of duty, undressed in the back of the truck and donned the skintight black suits they had been given by their superiors. The suits covered their entire bodies, head to toe, and were snug-fitting to minimize the slight blurring or visual distortion caused by an invisible object occupying space. Each suit had two pockets in which was a gun, flares to be used to signal for help, and a small pair of wire cutters for disarming explosive devices. A pair of goggles was secured over the eyes of each of the two to conceal their eyes. Once they were dressed, the Swiss lieutenant entered the back of the truck and used a small hose attached to a tank to spray them all over with Dr. Seward's invisibility mixture. Harker and Kopp watched each other vanish from sight!

Once it was done, Harker and Kopp climbed out of the back of the truck and began the last leg of the climb up to Blakely's house. Because they knew what to look for, they could—just barely—see where each other were by watching the distortion and by observing the leaves and snow being compressed under their feet. The suits, though tight, were thick and kept them warm in the alpine air. When they had gone on their way, the truck drove back down the mountain. It would soon return with eight policemen crammed in the back and three more stuffed in the front seat with the driver.

It was two o'clock in the afternoon when Harker and Kopp began their walk. The invisibility potion would wear off in three hours, so they had to be sure to complete their mission and signal for reinforcements by five. They walked quickly up the steep mountainside, but slowly enough to use adequate caution. They talked a bit as they proceeded.

"I can't seem to get used to this, to the strangeness of not being able to see you, or see myself," said Analiese Kopp. "You are not bothered by it, are you, Quincy?"

Harker shook his head, though he quickly realized that such a demonstrative gesture was futile since his companion could not see it. "I'll just say that I've grown used to some weirdness now and then. I've handled some unusual cases in my time, not to mention that such things seem to run in my family."

"In your family?" asked Kopp, "I'm not sure if I understand what you mean by that."

Harker's laughter cut through the chilly air and he had to remind himself that just because they couldn't be seen didn't mean they couldn't be heard. He lowered his voice. "I'm not quite sure what I mean by that either. Something strange happened to my parents before I was born...but they never spoke of it. Somehow I just knew that there was something there, some shadow in their memories that had made a lasting impression on the rest of their lives. It showed up in the little things, the habits they followed without even knowing it. I never asked them about it because I was afraid it would upset them. Nobody likes to be reminded of the bad times. Overall, I had a wonderful childhood, but sometimes I wish I knew what had happened to them all those years ago. Doctor Seward knows, I think. He was a family friend before I came into the world. I think he may even have been involved in whatever the 'incident' was, but I haven't really had the heart to ask him about it, either."

"You should ask him," suggested Inspector Kopp. "Everyone has a right to know something about their family history."

Harker decided it was his turn to ask a question. "What about you, Analiese? How did a girl like you wind up as a police inspector of all things? It's not exactly a standard profession for a woman."

There was only silence for half a minute, and then Harker heard Kopp's voice shake just a bit as she responded. "Ask me again sometime…when I've had a few drinks. It's not a favorite topic of mine. Let me just say that my choice of professions was motivated by a desire for revenge. Once I had accomplished that, I stuck with it. I liked it."

Harker let the subject rest. If she wanted to tell him more someday, he decided, she would choose the time and the place. He wondered if the story had anything to do with how she had gotten that scar on her face. They continued their walk up the mountain, talking less as they drew nearer to Blakely's home.

As the afternoon sun moved across the bright blue sky, Harker and Kopp, invisible to any nearby eyes, came to the place where Blakely's house rested atop the mountain. They looked at it from several hundred feet away. No one was visible outside the house, at least in the front.

"We'll work our way around the house, circle the building, see if we can spot any sign of all these explosives that Blakely bragged about," said Harker.

The two adventurers crept quietly around the entire perimeter of the property. Hope turned to disappointment as they saw that the entire home rested upon a raised cement foundation, leaving no space between the ground floor and the ground, at least no space that could be detected from the outside.

"If there are explosives," Analiese Kopp pointed out, "they must be beneath the building in a basement of some sort."

Harker, with an invisible hand, pulled back the edge of his invisible glove for a moment, glancing at the watch that lay hidden beneath the chemical-coated outer suit.

"Three-thirty," he said. "That gives us about ninety minutes more. We'll have to find a way inside."

"You said you leaped through the office window," Kopp recalled. "If they haven't repaired it yet, that could be a way in."

They found the place where Blakely's office looked out into the surrounding woods. The Swiss inspector's idea had been a fruitful one, as the window was now just a square hole with a sheet of cardboard covering it. Harker's invisible hand took his wire cutters from his pocket. Like a scene from a horror movie, the metal tool seemed to hover in the air, held aloft by Harker's invisible hand. He hoped that Blakely was not at his desk, behind the opaque sheet of cardboard. He poked a hole in the cardboard, placed the wire cutters back into his pocket, stuck his fingers into the hole, and tore the covering from the window. There was no reaction from inside, so he peered in. The office was empty. Inside his invisible mask, Harker smiled. "Let's go," he whispered to his companion.

They climbed through the window and walked across the empty office. Harker opened the door that led into the house's hallway. They entered that hallway and stopped to listen. In the distance, from another part of the house, they could hear voices. Harker knew that in one direction was the large room where Blakely conducted his experiments and kept his test subjects in locked cells that lined the walls. He decided to try the other direction. They proceeded down the hall, away from the sounds of the voices. They came to a door that Harker had never passed on his previous visit to Blakely's home. Kopp turned the knob and opened the door. Behind it they found a staircase leading down. In they went, slowly and carefully watching their step lest a slip of the foot or a sudden stumble should alert anyone of their invisible presence. At the bottom of the steps they found themselves in a basement that seemed to stretch for the entire length of the property. There were piles of crates stacked around the large space. They ignored the boxes and looked along the walls.

"Look!" said Kopp, pointing to the farthest wall of the cellar. Harker looked in the direction she indicated and saw, stacked four wide and four deep, crates that were marked with warning labels in bright red lettering, 'Highly Volatile!'

Running from the bottom crate was a wire which ran along the wall and disappeared into the ceiling, obviously connected to something on the main floor. Harker and Kopp walked for a closer look. Harker carefully lifted the top crate from the stack and gently placed it on the floor. He repeated the process with the next two crates until the bottom one of the left stack was uncovered. He lifted the lid from the bottom crate and he and Kopp looked inside. There was the wire coming into the crate from the outside, attached to a small device composed of other wires, an electrode, and various other components.

Harker let out a sigh. "I've never seen a detonator like this. I have no idea how to disarm this thing. Dammit!"

He felt the unseen hand of Analiese Kopp make contact with his forearm. "Leave this to me," she said, reassuringly. "Go upstairs and see what the situation is. I'll take care of the bomb." Her hand went into her pocket and out came her own wire cutters.

Harker chuckled. "You really are full of surprises, aren't you?"

To Harker's surprise, Kopp reached up and took off her goggles. Her eyes could be seen now, and Harker smiled at them floating like two blue stars in an otherwise empty sky. Then she reached up and pulled back her hood, revealing her face and letting her long blonde hair fall around her shoulders. She was smiling at Harker. "Let me see you before you go, Hound Dog," she said.

Harker pulled off his own goggles and hood. He pulled Analiese Kopp close to him and kissed her. Then he turned away, covered his head and eyes again, now invisible, and walked back to the staircase. Behind him, Analiese Kopp watched nothing walk away from her, hearing only the barely audible footsteps of what might as well have been a ghost. When she heard the door open and close again at the top of the stairs, she turned back to the mass of gizmos and wires and got to work.

Harker crept along the hallway. He wanted to find out where all the house's occupants were, what they were doing. He wanted to find Blakely and Jackal and Ernst and the other four former prisoners and see how Blakely's mad plot was progressing. Part of him knew he should have just stayed with Analiese and waited until she had defused the explosives and then left the house and signaled for help, but that just wasn't his way. He was too curious, too interested in the ways of madmen and their diabolical plots. He had to know, had to see things with his own eyes.

He went in the direction that he knew he would find the large room where he had seen Ernst forced to ingest Blakely's serum. He saw the door to that room up ahead and he was glad to see that it was open. He walked slowly and quietly to the doorway and peered inside, careful to make not a sound as he did not want to draw attention to his position, even if it was only with sound and not sight. Looking in, he saw two figures in the center of the room. Jackal sat on a chair by the table; he was smoking a cigar. The German giant, Ernst, was pacing behind him as if waiting impatiently for something. In the cells along the walls of the room sat the four other prisoners with whom Harker had traveled to the mountain, one to each cell, all looking dazed and drugged, probably the result of Blakely shooting them with his tranquilizing dart pistol. Harker stood there watching for several minutes. Neither Jackal nor Ernst seemed to be in the mood for conversation. Jackal smoked and Ernst paced. Both were silent. Harker wondered how Analiese Kopp was faring with the explosives detonator, and he wondered where Albert Blakely was.

It was four o'clock when Albert Blakely stepped out the front door of his house. He had been working all morning. Soon he would give another round of his red serum to his four caged test subjects. The big German, Ernst, had already had two doses and seemed to be handling its effects well. His aggressive personality, as well as his massively muscled physique, had responded to the serum, increasing his strength, stamina, and desire to go into terrible rages when prompted by Blakely or Jackal's orders. Hence, Blakely had seen no reason to keep that particular beast caged any longer. He hoped that the other four would soon be willing servants and soldiers of his as well.

He had decided to take a walk outside before proceeding with his work. All seemed to be going quite well for him, his plans coming together nicely, despite the recent interruption when the man called Arthur Quincy had escaped by throwing himself through a window and eventually killing the man called Rhino. Blakely did not think Quincy could have gone far and was certain that the defiant Englishman had died of exposure out there on the cold mountain. His body would eventually be found by skiers or local villagers and that would be the end of that matter.

Blakely breathed in the crisp, clean, cold mountain air and enjoyed the scenery around his home. He walked along the perimeter of the plot and around the back of the house. His mood was good...until he saw that the piece of cardboard, his makeshift window covering, had been torn asunder. He ran over to the window. He saw footprints, two pairs, one large and one smaller, in the snow and dirt below the now open window. He cursed out loud, though no one was close enough to hear him. He climbed in through the window and ran to the lab room where he knew his companions were. "Jackal, Jackal!" he shouted as he ran.

Quincy Harker heard the shouting and the footsteps from down the hall. He moved quickly to the side, invisible to all eyes, and watched as the panicked Albert Blakely darted past him into the room where all the other occupants of the house were.

Jackal jumped to his feet as Blakely entered.

"Jackal, Ernst...we are not alone here; someone has broken into our home! There are two of them! Jackal, search the basement! Ernst, take the main floor! I'll stay here with the prisoners and activate the explosives should it become necessary! We must not, under any circumstances, allow ourselves to be captured. Is that understood?"

Jackal and Ernst, in the manner of all brainwashed and willing slaves, simultaneously shouted, "Yes, sir!" and went on their way. Harker, stepping out of the path of traffic again, noted that Ernst was not armed, save for his gigantic fists, while Jackal had a revolver. He was tempted to pull out his gun and shoot them all where they were, but he did not. It would not be wise, he decided, to reveal his presence just yet. He decided that he should wait until Jackal and Ernst had left the immediate area, and then deal with Blakely before the madman could detonate those explosives, assuming that Inspector Kopp had not yet finished her disarming procedure.

As Jackal's and Ernst's footsteps faded down the long hallway, Harker readied himself for the confrontation. He felt for the gun in his pocket to be sure it was still there. It was, but while he felt for it he looked down, and gasped as he saw his own shoes! The invisibility potion was beginning to wear off! He watched as his ankles appeared; then his legs, his abdomen. Within seconds, he was completely visible again.

"You got me this far, Seward. Thanks, Doc!" he whispered, though Seward was miles away. Then he took out his gun and strode into the room.

In the basement of the house, Analiese Kopp had just cut the last wire. She was certain that she had successfully rendered the detonator useless. She let out a small sigh of relief, but it turned to a gasp as she saw the hand that was putting away her wire cutters, the hand that belonged to her. She realized that the chemical mixture had worn off. At the same moment, she heard the door at the top of the stairs open and footsteps approach. She judged them to be the steps of a man slightly lighter, somewhat shorter that Harker, so she drew her gun.

Jackal reached the bottom of the stairs and quickly, fluidly drew his weapon. He was about to pull the trigger when he suddenly stopped, stunned for just a second by the sight of a slim figure, clad from head to foot in a tightly fitted black suit with a pair of goggles over its eyes. That momentary hesitation was the end of Jackal. Analiese Kopp shot him, her dead aim putting a bullet through his heart.

A moment later, she regretted having fired that shot. She had given away her position, she knew. Now a much louder series of footsteps was coming down those stairs. She prepared herself to shoot whomever came into her sights next.

Ernst came barreling down the stairs. His face was twisted into a mask of fury and bloodlust. He was coming fast. Analiese Kopp shot him, but her aim was not so deadly as it had been when she sent Jackal to his grave moments before. The bullet struck Ernst in the shoulder, but it did not even slow down the raging hulk! Before the policewoman could fire another round, Ernst was right in front of her. He slapped the gun from her hand with his huge fist. His hand was hard as stone and Kopp yelped in pain as her wrist broke. She had no time even to grab her injured wrist with her other hand. Ernst grabbed her by the shoulders and picked her up off the floor. He tore the hood and goggles from her head, her blonde hair spilling down over her shoulders. Ernst stared at the pretty plaything he had found. The look in his bloodshot eyes was one of pure animal lust. Analiese Kopp screamed.

Harker walked into the room, his gun held out in front of him. Albert Blakely had seated himself by the table. His hand was under the table as if it waited to press a button or flip a switch of some kind. He looked up at the hooded, masked and goggled figure that had entered, gun in hand.

"Ah, Mr. Quincy," Blakely said. "It surprises me to see that you are not dead, although you have delayed that demise by only a few days."

Harker reached up and uncovered his head and face; there was no longer any need for the mask and hood. He tossed the headgear aside, the goggles clinking as they hit the floor.

"It's time to give up this silly scheme of yours, Blakely. The world is too big to be one man's property."

Blakely laughed. "I knew you weren't a true red-blooded Englishman, Mr. Quincy. A true Englishman would applaud my dream of a worldwide empire. It could have been glorious! Now I shall live in the history book, Mr. Quincy, not as a king, but as the shedder of many gallons of innocent blood. This mountain will shake and send death down upon the villagers below!"

Blakely's hand made a motion under the table. Harker heard the click of a switch...and then nothing happened. Blakely just stared for a moment, and then he roared, a primal, angry, bitter scream of pain, disappointment, insanity! Harker cringed at the sound, seeing how pathetic and unbalanced Blakely really was. It was the sound of a once brilliant mind unhinged by delusion and greed. The terrible sound faded away, but it was soon replaced by an equally horrifying sound: the sound of a female scream, shrill, terrified, helpless.

Harker had had enough of Albert Blakely. His mind turned to Analiese Kopp and her bloodcurdling scream. He knew he had to get to her as quickly as he could. She was not the type of woman who could be easily made to scream like that.

Harker knew he had to be done with Blakely before he could safely leave the room and see to Kopp. He fired one shot from his gun, hitting Blakely in the chest. The megalomaniac chemist slumped down in his chair without a sound. Harker did not like to kill so mercilessly, but he had no choice. He turned his back on Blakely and ran out into the hall.

He went first to the front door, taking the flare gun from his pocket as he ran. He flung the door open, fired the flare into the sky, and turned back inside. He raced to the door with the staircase behind it and flew down the stairs, tossing the flare gun aside and readying his real pistol again.

Down the mountain, the waiting police saw the flare explode in the sky above. The lieutenant who was driving began to speed the truck up the steep mountain road. The men in the passenger seat and in the back prepared for whatever they might find when they reached the top.

Harker reached the bottom of the staircase. He was greeted by the sight of the towering form of Ernst, all exaggerated muscle and growling insanity, holding up the small, fragile form of Analiese Kopp with one hand around her throat. With his other hand he was tearing the tight black suit from her body like a hungry ape might peel a banana. Kopp's face was an expression of pure terror.

Harker thought about shooting the huge German in the back, but he feared that his bullet might strike Analiese. He tossed the gun to the floor and threw himself at Ernst. The monstrous killer dropped the girl and turned his attention to Harker. He fell on top of the British captain and raised a powerful fist to land a crushing blow to Harker's head. The fist came down, but Harker rolled to the side. The fist hit bare floor with a loud thud. Harker raised his own fist, slamming his knuckles into Ernst's windpipe. Ernst grabbed his injured throat, coughing and choking!

Harker struggled to get out from under the choking Ernst. Try as he might, he could not lift the massive German off. Ernst's hands came off his own throat and wrapped around Harker's neck, squeezing hard, strangling him. Harker could feel his air being cut off, could see darkness beginning to close in around the borders of his vision. For one of the few times in his life of adventure, Harker was actually afraid.

Analiese Kopp struggled to stand. She had sat on the floor where Ernst had dropped her. Her clothing hung from her body in shreds; her wrist was broken and her hand hung limply, throbbing with terrible pain. She could have sat and cried, but she chose to focus her anger instead, let her rage build up and take over her thoughts. She stood and walked over to where Harker had dropped his gun. She picked it up, walked over to where Ernst kneeled over the nearly unconscious Harker. Analiese Kopp took aim, focused on her anger, and put a bullet in the murderous German's head.

Albert Blakely opened his eyes. He groaned once in pain and remembered where he was. That man, that traitor, Arthur Quincy had shot him, but he was still alive. Blakely swore to himself that he would not die; he would live on, rebuild his laboratory and continue his plans to rule the world. He had the means to survive this day, he told himself. That means was right there in his pocket. Ignoring the pain, ignoring the blood that seeped from his bullet wound, he reached into his pocket and took out a small vial of red liquid. His left arm was numb, but his right hand functioned. He raised the vial, used his teeth to remove the stopper, and drank the red serum down in one bitter gulp.

Blakely felt a strange intoxicating sensation surging through his body and his mind; the pain was gone, his will and his strength were returning. He stood. He felt incredible! He ran out of the room, down the hallway, to the front door of his house on top of the world. He tore open the front door, ran out into the snowy land, raised his arms to the sky and shouted at the top of his lungs, "The world will be mine!"

An instant later, Albert Blakely was riddled with bullets simultaneously launched from the guns of twelve Swiss police officers. The snow was stained with crimson liquid. This time, only a small portion of that redness came from Blakely's strange elixir. The rest had run through his veins.

Three days later, Captain Quincy Harker walked, once again, out of a hospital in Geneva. He had not been seriously hurt at Blakely's home, but since he had nearly been strangled to death, the doctors had insisted that he stay for observation. It had been a long, boring three days, but they had finally agreed to release him. Now he walked out onto the streets of Geneva, lighting a cigarette and noticing that the air seemed a bit warmer than it had when he had arrived in Switzerland.

Colonel Sharpe, Doctor Seward, and Picky Pickover had already flown back to London. Sharpe had other matters to attend to, Seward had wanted to get back to Clarice, and Pickover—although he had wanted to stay with Harker—had been told to go back. Now Harker looked forward to the one-week's leave that Sharpe had granted him after the successful completion of the case. He looked forward to being away from his usual surroundings while not on a case, and he looked forward to being almost, but not completely, alone.

"Oh, there you are, Quincy," said a voice from behind him. The voice sounded gentler, more feminine than it had when its owner had been on duty. Harker turned to see Analiese Kopp standing there. Her arm was in a sling and her face was a bit bruised, but her hair was down and her expression was less serious than the policewoman-on-the-job face she usually wore. She smiled at Harker and they walked down the Geneva street together.

WATSON'S
WILD WEST

You'll excuse me if I have a hard time wrapping my mind around the fact that another year has actually flown by. It only seemed like just yesterday that I was writing the Afterward to our very first Dr. Watson solo adventure, SEASON OF MADNESS, by Aaron Smith. It was our fondest hope at that time to do more of the good doctor's solo adventures and, lo and behold, along comes Erwin K. Roberts with a dandy tale that completely fulfilled that wish.

Roberts has detailed how he came to write this particular tale in his own Author's Epilog, allow me to add my own thoughts on why this particular story excited me so much. Never mind that Watson is a great character in his own right, and hopefully this series will add to his stature as Holmes' qualified equal, but this story had him crossing paths with one of the most remarkable men in all of history, Theodore Roosevelt. Both yours truly and art director, Rob Davis, are Roosevelt enthusiasts. Which is interesting as Rob is a liberal Democrat and I'm a registered Republican. It is obvious there was something apolitical about Teddy's brand of Americanism and patriotism that reaches across the right and left aisles of our philosophies even to this day.

One of the classic hallmarks of any good pulp story is an exotic, colorful locale. When Watson arrives in New York City at the turn of the century and then ultimately makes his way west with Roosevelt as his guide, I was sold. So was Rob when I suggested the wonderful cover that now adorns this volume, with spectacular finishing colors by Shane Evans; it is an image worth framing. Shane has graced many Airship 27 covers and we hope many more to come.

The final icing on the cake was having Aaron Smith deliver another exciting chapter in the exploits of his own creation, Her Majesty's Secret Service Agent, Quincy "Hound Dog" Harker. It is our plan to have a new Hound Dog Harker as a bonus treat in every Dr. Watson we are fortunate enough to bring you.

So there you have it. Airship 27 Productions plans to start each year with a brand new *Sherlock Holmes – Consulting Detective* anthology and close out each year with a solo Dr. Watson adventure.[1] We think they make great literary bookends to our exciting pulp offerings that are sandwiched in between and hope you concur. 2011 is looming over the horizon and as always we thank you so much for your continued support throughout 2010. We've lots of great new titles heading your way in the next twelve months.

As always, we cordially invite you to visit our on-line store (http://www.airship27hangar.com/). There you'll find all our thrilling, action-packed books.

Ron Fortier
10/16/2010
Fort Collins, Co.
(Airship27@comcast.net)
(www.Airship27.com)

---

1   **Editor's note**: This volume was originally intended for publication at the end of 2010. A number of factors led to the book being delayed to its present release in the middle of 2012. We hope you think, as we do, that the wait was worth it.

THE BAKER STREET SLEUTH RETURNS

The best selling series continues here with Volume III of "Sherlock Holmes – Consulting Detective" and presents a brand new quintet of terrific, classic Holmes mysteries written in the tradition of his creator; Sir Arthur Conan Doyle.

Five brand new puzzles to challenge the Great Detective and his ever loyal companion, Dr.Watson. Within these pages they will encounter mythological fairies seeming to plague a beautiful country estate, man-eating tigers on the loose in the streets of London and a stolen museum mummy. These are only some of the mysteries awaiting the famous crime solving duo as penned by today's most gifted writers; Aaron Smith, I.A. Watson, Joshua Reynolds and Andrew Salmon. Both Salmon & Watson having won the prestigious Pulp Factory Award for their earlier Holmes tales in volumes one and two respectively.

Airship 27 Productions is thrilled to be continuing this extremely popular series which Sherlock Holmes fans around the globe have made an overwhelming success. Volume III features a wonderful new cover painting by Brian McCulloch plus eleven interior illustrations by the book's designer, Rob Davis, another Pulp Factory Award winner for his work on volume one. So load your revolvers, hail a hansom and prepare yourself for page turning thrills aplenty. Once again, the game is afoot!

PULP FICTION FOR A NEW GENERATION!

AVAILABLE AT BOOKSTORES WORLD-WIDE, AT AMAZON.COM ONLINE AND AS A PDF EBOOK AT: Airship27hangar.com

AN AIRSHIP 27 PRODUCTION

NEW **PULP**

The Return of Baron Gruner

In 1902 Sir James Damery enlisted the aid of Sherlock Holmes to prevent the daughter of an old friend from marrying a womanizing Austrian named Adelbert Gruner who was suspected of murdering his first wife. Dr. Watson chronicled the case as "The Adventure of the Illustrious Client." By its conclusion, Gruner's evil intent was exposed to the young lady when Holmes came into possession of an album listing his many amorous conquests. A former prostitute mistress of the Baron's then took her own revenge by throwing acid in his face – permanently disfiguring him.

Holmes believed the matter concluded. He is proven wrong when a hideous murder occurs rife with evidence indicating the Baron has returned. Soon the Great Detective will learn he has been targeted for revenge in a cruel and sadistic fashion. Not only does the Baron wish his death but he is obsessed with causing Holmes emotional suffering. He desires nothing less that the complete and utter destruction of the Great Detective in body and soul.

Gary Lovisi spins a fast paced tale of horror and intrigue that is both suspenseful and poignant, all the while remaining true to Arthur Conan Doyle's original stories. "The Baron's Revenge" is a thrilling sequel to a classic Holmes adventure fans will soon be applauding.

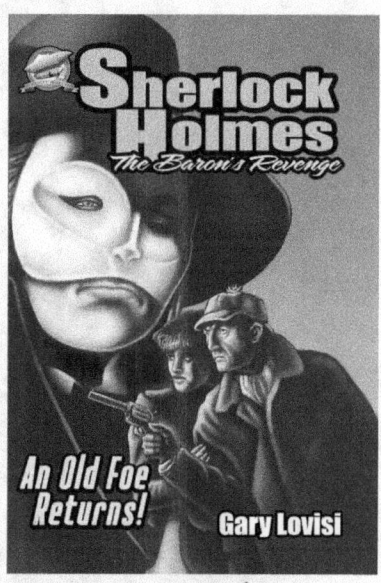

Sherlock Holmes
The Baron's Revenge

An Old Foe Returns!

Gary Lovisi

www.ingramcontent.com/pod-product-compliance
Lightning Source LLC
Chambersburg PA
CBHW071240250626

47163CB00001B/263